MARY DOWNING HAHN

The Ghost of Crutchfield Hall

CLARION BOOKS
HOUGHTON MIFFLIN HARCOURT
BOSTON   NEW YORK   2010

CLARION BOOKS
215 Park Avenue South
New York, New York 10003

The text of this book is set in 12.5-point Franklin Caslon.
Book design by Sharismar Rodriguez

Clarion Books is an imprint of Houghton Mifflin Harcourt Publishing Company.

www.hmhbooks.com

Library of Congress Cataloging-in-Publication Data

Hahn, Mary Downing.
The ghost of Crutchfield Hall / by Mary Downing Hahn.
p. cm.
Summary: In the nineteenth century, twelve-year-old Florence Crutchfield leaves a London
orphanage to live with her great-uncle, great-aunt, and sickly cousin James, but she soon
realizes the home has another resident, who means to do her and James harm.
ISBN 978-0-547-38560-0
[1. Orphans—Fiction. 2. Ghosts—Fiction. 3. Brothers and sisters—Fiction. 4. Jealousy—
Fiction. 5. Great Britain—History—Victoria, 1837–1901—Fiction.] I. Title.

PZ7.H1256Gho 2010
[Fic]—dc22

2009045351

Manufactured in the United States of America

DOC 10 9 8 7 6 5 4 3 2 1
4500237149

For my daughters, Kate and Beth,
who will always be my favorite readers

ဢ

ONE

"TAKE GOOD CARE OF THIS GIRL," Miss Beatty told the coachman. "She's an orphan, you know, and never set foot out of London. Make sure she gets where she's going safely."

After turning to me, Miss Beatty smoothed my hair and checked the note she'd pinned to my coat: "Mistress Florence Crutchfield," it read. "Bound for Crutchfield Hall, near Lower Bolton."

"Now, you behave yourself," she warned me. "Don't talk to strangers, no matter how nice they seem, sit still, and don't daydream. Keep your mind on what you're doing and where you're going." She paused and dabbed her eyes with her handkerchief.

"And when you get to your uncle's house . . ." She sniffed and went on, "Be a good girl. Do as you're bid. None of your mischief, or he'll be sending you back here."

Unable to restrain myself, I threw my arms around her. "I'll miss you."

Miss Beatty stiffened a moment, as if unaccustomed to being embraced. Certainly I'd never had the nerve to do so before.

"Now, now—no tears." She gave me a quick hug, then stepped back as if she'd done something wrong. Affection of any sort was not encouraged at Miss Medleycoate's Home for Orphan Girls. "Remember your manners, Florence. Always say please and thank you, and don't slurp your soup."

"Is that girl coming with us or not?" the coachman asked.

"Go along then, Florence." Miss Beatty gave me a gentle push toward the coach. As a passenger held out his hand to assist me, she said softly, "I pray you'll be happy in your new home."

Once inside the coach, I looked out the window just in time to glimpse Miss Beatty's broad back vanish into the crowd in the coach yard. The last I saw of her was the big yellow flower on her hat. She was the only grownup at Miss Medleycoate's Home for Orphan Girls who'd treated me—or any of us—with kindness.

On his rooftop seat, the coachman cracked his whip, and away we went, bouncing over cobbled streets and rattling through parts of London I'd never seen. I glimpsed the Tower, the dome of St. Paul's Cathedral, and mazes of twisting alleyways. Then we hurtled across Tower Bridge and into the narrow streets of Southwark, crowded with coaches, wagons, and people, all doing their best to move onward at the expense of everyone else.

In the crowded coach, I was squashed between a large redheaded woman and an even larger gentleman with a beard that threatened to scratch my cheek if I was jostled too close to him.

Directly opposite me sat a narrow-faced young man with a mustache and a wispy beard, attempting to read his Bible. Next to him a rough-looking fellow frowned and scowled at all of us. Making herself as small as possible, a timid lady with gray hair and spectacles pressed herself against the side of the coach.

Before five minutes had passed, the gentleman beside me fell asleep and commenced to snore loudly. On my other side, the stout woman fussed to herself and even went so far as to reach across me and poke the sleeper with her umbrella. She failed to rouse him.

Across from me, the rough fellow began a conversation with the Bible reader, which soon turned into an argument about Mr. Darwin's theory of evolution— the Bible reader for and the rough fellow against. The old lady closed her eyes and either fell asleep or feigned to.

The woman beside me opined that she was not descended from apes, no matter what Mr. Darwin had thought. She did not, however, voice her opinion loudly enough to be heard by the Bible reader and the rough fellow.

While all this went on about me, I mused upon the sudden change in my circumstances. My parents had drowned in a boating accident when I was five years old. When no relative stepped forward to claim me, I was sent to Miss Medleycoate's, where I spent seven wretched years learning to sew and read and write from a series of strict teachers who had little patience with girls who could not stitch a neat row or learn their arithmetic. We were cold in the winter, hot in the summer, and hungry all year round. If we dared to complain, we were beaten and locked in the punishment closet.

Then one day, just a week ago, a solicitor appeared at the orphanage and informed Miss Medleycoate that I was the great-niece of Thomas Crutchfield, my father's uncle. My uncle had searched for me a long time and had finally learned my whereabouts. As soon as proper arrangements were made, Mr. Graybeale said, I was to live at Crutchfield Hall with my uncle, his spinster sister, Eugenie, and my cousin James, the orphaned son of my father's only brother.

Glancing around the dreary sitting room, Mr. Graybeale had told me I was a fortunate girl.

"She certainly is." Miss Medleycoate fixed me with a sharp eye. "I am certain Florence will show her gratitude as she has been taught."

I knew full well how fortunate I was to escape Miss Medleycoate's establishment, but I merely bowed my head to avoid her stare. Now was not the time to express my feelings.

"What sort of boy is my cousin James?" I asked Mr. Graybeale. "Is he my age? Is he—"

"I've never met the child," Mr. Graybeale said, "but I hear he's rather delicate."

I stared at the solicitor, wondering what he meant. "Is he sickly?"

"Florence," Miss Medleycoate interrupted. "Do

not pester the gentleman with trivial questions. Your curiosity does not become you."

"It's all right," Mr. Graybeale told Miss Medleycoate. Turning to me, he said, "The boy has suffered much in his short life. His mother died soon after he was born, and his father succumbed to a fever a few years later. Not long after James and his older sister, Sophia, arrived at Crutchfield Hall, the girl was killed in a tragic accident. So much loss has been difficult for James to bear."

I stared at Mr. Graybeale. "I'm so sorry," I whispered. Perhaps I should not have asked about James's health, but if I had not, how would I have known about my cousin's tragic past and Sophia's death? Disturbing as these events were, I needed to be aware of them, if only to avoid asking my aunt and uncle inappropriate questions.

With a rustle of silk, Miss Medleycoate rose to her feet. "I believe Mr. Graybeale has satisfied your unseemly curiosity, Florence. You may return to your lessons while I sign the necessary papers."

Now, as the coach bounced and swayed over rough roads, I thought about Sophia. If only she hadn't died, if only she were waiting for me at Crutchfield

Hall, the friend I'd always wanted, the sister I'd never had.

I imagined us whispering and giggling together, sharing books and games and dolls, telling each other secrets. We'd sleep in the same room and talk to each other in the dark. We'd go for long walks in the country. She'd show me her favorite things—a creek that swirled over white pebbles, lily pads in a pond, a bird's nest, butterflies, a tree with branches low enough to sit on and read. Maybe we'd have a dog or a pony.

Suddenly the coach hit a bump with enough force to hurl me against the man beside me. He drew away and scowled, as if offended by my proximity. Brought back to the stuffy confines of reality, I let go of my daydream. Sophia would not be waiting for me at Crutchfield Hall. I would have no sister. Just James, delicate James, a brother who might not be well enough to play.

With a sigh, I reminded myself that I was a fortunate girl. With every turn of the coach's wheels, I was leaving Miss Medleycoate's Home for Orphan Girls farther and farther behind. Surely I'd be happier at Crutchfield Hall than I'd been with Miss Medleycoate.

Two

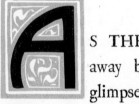

S THE CITY SLOWLY FADED away behind us, I caught fleeting glimpses of open countryside, green meadows rolling away toward distant hills, red-roofed villages marked by church steeples, cows and sheep under a cloudy sky much higher and wider than it looked in London. I felt very small, rather like an ant riding in a coach the size of a walnut shell.

After an hour or so, the sky darkened and the wind rose. Rain pelted the coach and streamed down the windows, making it impossible to see out.

We stopped several times to let passengers off and take more on. The rough fellow was replaced by a farmer who had nothing to say to anyone. The old lady was replaced by a young woman who blushed whenever anyone looked at her.

The coach grew stuffy, and the voices around me blended into a sort of soothing music. The jolts and bumps and lurches changed to a rocking motion, and I soon fell asleep.

I was startled awake by the large woman beside me. "Stir yourself, child. This is where you get off."

"Crutchfield Hall," the coachman bellowed from his seat above us. "Ain't there someone what wants to get out here?"

I scrambled to my feet and stepped outside. Wind and rain struck me with a force that almost knocked me down. Groggy with sleep, I gazed at empty fields bordered by a forest, bare and bleak on this dark January afternoon. In the distance, I saw a line of hills, their tops hidden by rain, but no house. Not even a barn or a shed.

Bewildered, I peered up at the coachman through the rain. "Where is the house, sir?"

Gesturing with his whip, he pointed to an ornate iron gate topped with fancy curlicues. "Follow the drive till you come to the house," he said. "It's one or two mile, I reckon. A big old place with chimneys. Pity there's no one to meet you."

With that, he handed me the small wooden box that held all my belongings. "Be sure and latch the gate behind you," he said. "They won't like it left open."

Before I could say another word, he cracked his whip. In seconds, the coach vanished into the rain.

With a sigh, I lowered my head and pushed open the heavy gate, then latched it behind me. The rain came down harder. The wind sent volleys of leaves flying against my face, as sharp edged as small knives.

Frightened by the creaking and groaning of tree limbs over my head, I walked faster, almost losing my shoes in the mud. They were thin soled, meant for city streets, not country lanes. I supposed I was meant for city streets as well, for I did not like the vast sky above me. The endless fields and the distant hills made me feel as if I were the only living person in this desolate place.

I was tempted to turn around and walk back to the road. Perhaps another coach would come along, warm and crowded with passengers, and take me back to London's familiar streets.

But I kept going, fearing Miss Medleycoate would not accept me. Had she not been happy to see me leave? I did not want to end my days begging in the street.

Finally, ankle deep in mud and soaked by the rain, I came to the top of a hill. Below me was a gloomy stone house, grim and unwelcoming, its windows dark and lifeless. Except for a dense grove of fir trees, the gardens and lawn were brown and bare.

A writer like Miss Emily Brontë would have been entranced by its Gothic appearance, but I hung back again, suddenly apprehensive of what might await me behind those towering walls.

It was the rising wind and icy rain that drove me forward. Exhausted and cold, I made my way carefully downhill to the house. In the shelter of a stone arch, I lifted an iron ring and let it thud against the door. Shivering in my wet coat and sodden shoes, I waited for someone to come.

Just as I was about to knock again, I heard footsteps approaching. The door slowly opened. A tall, thin woman dressed in black looked down at me. Her face was pale and narrow, her eyes were set deep under her brows, and her gray hair was pulled tightly into a bun at the back of her head. With a gasp, she pressed one bony hand to her heart. "It cannot be," she whispered. "It cannot be."

Fearing she was about to faint, I took her cold

hand. "I-I'm Florence Crutchfield," I stammered. "From London. I believe you're expecting me."

She snatched her hand away and looked at me more closely. "For a moment I mistook you for someone else," she murmured, her voice still weak. "But now I see you bear no resemblance to her. None at all."

Without inviting me in, the woman said, "We were told you'd arrive tomorrow."

"I beg your pardon, but Miss Medleycoate said I was to come today." Panic made my heart beat faster. "She said I was to come today," I repeated. "*Today.*"

At that moment, an old gentleman appeared in the shadowy hallway. The very opposite of the woman, he was short and round, and his cheeks were rosy with good humor. In one hand he held a pipe and in the other a thick book. "Come in," he said to me, "come in. You're wet and cold."

To the woman he said, "This poor child must be our great-niece Florence. Why have you allowed her to stand on the doorstep, shivering like a half-drowned kitten?"

"You know my feelings about her coming here." Without another word, she turned stiffly and vanished into the house's gloomy interior.

Puzzled by my aunt's unfriendly manner, I followed my uncle down the hall. What had I done to cause Aunt to dislike me almost on sight?

"As you must have guessed," my uncle said, "I'm your Great-Uncle Thomas, and that was my sister, your Great-Aunt Eugenie. I apologize for her brusqueness. I'm sure she didn't mean to be rude. She, er, she . . ."

Uncle paused as if searching for the right words to describe his sister. "Well," he went on, "once she becomes accustomed to you, she'll be friendlier. Yes, yes, you'll see. She just has to get used to you."

I didn't dare ask how long it would take Aunt to get used to me. Or how long it would take *me* to get used to *her*. Indeed, I felt I had escaped Miss Medleycoate only to encounter her double. Which was neither what I'd hoped for nor what I'd expected.

"And then of course," Uncle went on, "we really did expect you to arrive tomorrow. I'd have sent Spratt to meet you if I'd known you'd arrive today. A misunderstanding on someone's part, but, well, what's done is done. I am very happy to see you."

Uncle led me into a large room lit by flickering firelight and oil lamps. Rain beat against its small windows, and the wind crept through every crack around the glass panes, but I felt cheered by the fire's glow and my uncle's smile.

"Here, let me have a look at you." Uncle grasped my shoulders and peered into my face. "Goodness, Eugenie, have you noticed how much she favors the Crutchfields? Blue eyes, dark hair—she could be Sophia's sister."

My aunt frowned at me from a chair by the hearth. "Don't be absurd. This girl is quite plain. And her hair is a sight."

Busying myself with my coat buttons, I pretended not to have heard Aunt. I didn't know what Sophia looked like, but I was quite ready to believe she was much prettier than I. Aunt was right. I was plain. And my hair was tangled by the wind and wet with rain and no doubt a sight.

Uncle took my sodden coat and settled me near the fire. "You must be tired and cold," he said. "You've had a long, muddy walk from the road." He picked up a bell and rang it.

A girl not much older than I popped into the room as if she'd been waiting by the door. She was so thin, she'd wrapped her apron strings twice around her waist, but the apron still flapped around her like a windless sail.

"Nellie," my uncle said, "this is Florence, the niece we expected to arrive tomorrow. Please bring tea for us all and something especially nice for Florence. Then build up the fire in her room."

Darting a quick look in my direction, Nellie nodded. "Yes, sir, I will, sir."

As she scurried away, Uncle turned back to me. "First of all, permit me to say how sorry I was to learn of your father's and mother's death. To think they died on the same day. So tragic. So unexpected."

"Sensible people do not go out in boats," Aunt said, and then, with a quick glance at me, added, "Death is usually unexpected. That is why we must endeavor to live righteously. When we are summoned, we will be ready. As Sophia was, poor child."

Ignoring his sister, Uncle patted my hand. "We'll do our best to make up for the years you spent with Miss Medleycoate. You'll have a happy life here at Crutchfield Hall, I promise you."

I did not say it, but the prospect of a happy life with Aunt seemed uncertain at best.

As Uncle drew in his breath to say more, he was

interrupted by the arrival of Nellie, who carried a heavy tray. In its center was a steaming teapot, which was surrounded by an array of sliced bread, cheese, and fruit, as well as milk and sugar for the tea and jam for the bread. Somehow she managed to set it down on a low table by the fire without rattling a teacup in its saucer.

I hadn't eaten since breakfast, and my empty stomach mortified me by rumbling at the sight of so much food, more than I'd ever seen at the orphanage. At that establishment, we received one cup of tea served lukewarm and weak, a slice of stale bread, and a dab of jelly.

Nellie's eyes met mine again, but she didn't linger. With a nod, she left the room, her feet scarcely making a sound.

Uncle offered me the bread and jam. "Don't be shy," he said. "Take as much as you want. Walking in the cold sharpens one's appetite."

While we ate, I looked around the room. Despite its darkness, I saw it was well furnished with chairs and sofas and shelves of books. Oil paintings covered the walls. Some were portraits of long-ago men and women, their faces grave in the firelight. Others were landscapes of forested hills and grassy meadows. A marble statue of a Greek god stood in the corner behind Aunt's chair, peering over her shoulder as if hoping for a biscuit.

"And now, my dear," Uncle said, "tell us about yourself. Do you play an instrument? Sing? Draw? What sort of books do you enjoy?"

"I'm sorry to say I don't play a musical instrument," I told him. "Neither do I sing. Indeed, my talents in music resemble those of Mary Bennet in *Pride and*—"

"How unfortunate," Aunt cut in. "Your cousin Sophia played the piano *and* the violin. She sang like an angel. Such talent she had, such grace." Her voice trailed away, and she sniffed into her handkerchief.

"You were about to say something more," Uncle prompted me.

Embarrassed by my inferiority to Sophia, I murmured, "I was just going to say that I draw a little. Not very well, I'm afraid."

With a worried look at Aunt, I hesitated. "As for books," I went on nervously, "I love Mr. Dickens's novels, and also those of Wilkie Collins. I've read all of Jane Austen's books, but my favorite is *Pride and Prejudice*, which I've read five times now. I adore *Wuthering Heights* and—"

"Do you read nothing but frivolous novels?" Aunt cut in. "I have read the Bible at least a dozen times, but I have not read *Pride and Prejudice* even once. Nor do I intend to. As for Mr. Dickens—I believe him to be most vulgar. Wilkie Collins is beneath contempt. And the Brontë novel is quite the worst of the lot, not fit for a decent young girl to read."

Her tone of voice and stern face silenced me. I fancied even the clock on the mantel had ceased ticking.

Aunt peered at me over the top of her spectacles. "If the Bible is too difficult for you," she added, "I recommend *Pilgrim's Progress*. It should prove most instructive. Your cousin Sophia told me it was her favorite book." Then, without saying farewell or making an excuse for her departure, she left the room.

When the door closed behind her, Uncle sighed. "Your aunt is very set in her ways, I fear," he said. "You may read what you wish. I for one see nothing wrong with your taste in literature. Dickens is my own personal favorite. *Martin Chuzzlewit, Bleak House, Our Mutual Friend*—ah, what untold hours of pleasure his books have given me."

I tried to return his smile, but I feared I'd made a poor beginning with Aunt. "I didn't mean to offend my aunt."

"Don't worry. She'll come round." He set his teacup down. "She was very fond of Sophia, you know. Absolutely doted on the girl. Still wears nothing but black."

"Sophia must have been perfection itself," I said sadly.

"No one is perfect, my dear. Certainly not Sophia." He picked up his tea as if to end the conversation.

I sat quietly, sipping my tea and listening to the incessant sound of the wind and the rain. The journey had exhausted me, and I tried without success to stifle a yawn.

Uncle looked at me and smiled. "Perhaps you'd like to rest and refresh yourself before supper."

"Will James join us?" I asked. "I was hoping he'd be here for tea. I can scarcely wait to meet him."

Uncle sighed again. "James is quite ill, my dear. He never leaves his room."

Before I could say another word, Uncle summoned Nellie. "Please show Florence to her room," he said. "She's tired from her long day of travel."

Almost too weary to walk, I followed Nellie up a wide flight of stairs to the second floor. She opened a door at the end of a hall and led me into a room almost as large as the dormitory where I'd slept with eleven girls. A coal fire glowed on the hearth, filling the room with warmth.

As Nellie busied herself lighting an oil lamp, I contemplated my new surroundings. A tall four-poster bed wide enough to hold three girls my size. Bookcases, chests, bureaus, a tall wardrobe, all made of dark wood, massive, designed for giants. I felt like Alice after she drank the shrinking potion.

Under a curtained window was a writing table and a chair, a perfect place to read and draw.

Lamp lit, Nellie looked at me shyly. "Supper will be served at seven, miss."

After the girl left, I took off my wet shoes and stockings and lay for a while on my bed, staring up at the canopy above. Finally, too restless to sleep, I went to the window and pulled the curtains aside. Night had fallen while we'd had tea, and darkness and rain prevented me from seeing anything except a few bare trees close to the house. There were no lights in sight. To one accustomed to the busy streets of London, it was a bleak and lonely view.

Chilled by the draft creeping in around the window frames, I closed the curtains and retreated to the warmth of the fire.

Shortly before seven, I pulled on a pair of dry stockings and forced my feet back into my damp shoes, the only ones I owned. I wished I had a nicer dress, but I was wearing my best, a simple frock meant for church. My only other was the orphanage uniform made of coarse material, and a bit small for me. I did what I could with my hair, a wild mass of dark, curly tangles, and left my room.

At the top of the stairs, I had the strangest sensation that someone was watching me. I looked behind me. The hall was dark, and even though I saw no one, the sensation persisted. A chill raced up and down my spine, and my scalp prickled. "Is someone there?" I whispered fearfully.

I heard a faint sound like muffled laughter.

"Nellie, is that you?"

The laughter faded. The watcher was gone and I was alone.

Almost tripping over my own feet, I ran downstairs as if I were being chased.

THREE

B Y THE TIME I REACHED THE dining room, my heart had slowed to its normal speed. I told myself sternly that no one had been watching me. No one had laughed. I'd been a silly child scared of my own shadow.

Uncle rose from his seat at the table and greeted me warmly. "It will be just the two of us tonight," he said. "Eugenie is indisposed and will not join us."

"Oh, dear, I'm sorry to hear that," I said as graciously as I could. "I hope it's not my fault."

"No, indeed," Uncle assured me. "It's merely a spot of dyspepsia. Nervous stomach, Dr. Fielding says. She's high strung, you know. Nervy."

I nodded sympathetically, but even though I knew it was uncharitable, I hoped Aunt's condition would cause her to miss many meals.

The two of us sat across from each other at the end of a long table covered with a spotless white cloth and set with fine china, crystal, and silver. A blazing candelabra illuminated the table, but the rest of the room lay deep in shadow.

I'd never eaten in such surroundings, and I was suddenly nervous about my manners. Which fork to use first? Which spoon? There were so many utensils to choose from.

Nellie brought our meal. Giving me her usual quick, curious look, she served us each a plate of roast chicken, potatoes, and carrots. With a nod to Uncle, she left the room.

Watching my uncle closely, I chose the same utensils he did and tried my best to demonstrate I knew proper etiquette.

While we ate, Uncle told me about Crutchfield Hall. "It was built in the early 1700s by my great-grandfather, not so old or so big as some country houses, but more than ample for our needs at the present."

He paused to eat a forkful of potatoes and then

went on. "Not many servants now either. Mrs. Dawson does the cooking, and Samuel Spratt tends the grounds. Nellie is the maid—a jack-of-all-trades, you could call her. Once a week Mrs. Barnes comes in from the village to do the heavy cleaning. We used to have a larger staff, but we get along fine without them."

As Uncle helped himself to more chicken, I summoned the courage to ask what I really wanted to know. "When will I meet James?"

"I can't really say. Your aunt doesn't think he's well enough for you to visit him. It would tire him, she claims." While he spoke, Uncle rolled his silver napkin holder back and forth on the tablecloth.

"What sort of illness does he have?" I asked. "Will he always be an invalid?"

Uncle shook his head. "Dr. Fielding is as puzzled as I am. It's as if the boy wants to be sick. He told me once that it suits him to lie in bed all day."

"How sad." I wished I could think of something else to say, but I couldn't imagine why any child would prefer sickness to health. I hated staying in bed. I detested fevers and aches and pains and upset stomachs. I abhorred coughing and sneezing and blowing my nose.

"Yes, it is indeed sad." Without looking at me, Uncle continued to roll his napkin holder back and forth, as if it were a little wheel engaged in an important task. "After his sister's death, the boy went into a long decline. Sometimes I think he blames himself . . ." Unable to go on, he pulled a handkerchief out of his pocket and blew his nose.

Embarrassed by his obvious distress, I lowered my head. Despite my earlier promise to myself, I'd asked the wrong questions, upset my uncle, and had no idea what to say to make amends.

For the rest of our meal, we ate quietly. Uncle did not mention James again, nor did he speak of Sophia.

After supper, we sat by the sitting room fire and read. Uncle's book was thick and heavy. I made out the name Thomas Carlyle on the spine. I'd never read him, but I had a feeling his writings might be a bit tedious.

Hoping to find something more interesting, I searched the shelves until I found *Great Expectations*. I'd read it three times already, but I was happy to be reunited with my old friend Pip, especially here, so far from my playmates at the orphanage.

When the clock struck nine, I said good night to Uncle and went up to bed. I did not linger at the top of the steps but went quickly to my room and closed the door firmly.

Used to sleeping in a roomful of girls, I lay alone in the dark and tried to accustom myself to the silence. No one breathed or sighed or sniffled. No one turned and tossed. No one coughed. No one sobbed into her pillow.

I watched the coals smolder in the grate. Little blue flames flickered here and there but did not cast much light. The wind rose and made an eerie sound at the window. Drafts of cold air stirred the curtains and crept under my covers.

Unable to sleep, I gave up and went to my window. The wind had swept away the rain, and a full moon floated high in the sky, dodging clouds. How vast and empty the land was. Fields and hills, turned silver and black by the moon's light, rolled away into the hills beyond. Beautiful as it was, the solitude frightened me. I longed for lighted windows and chimneys, for voices and the clippety-clop of horses in the street.

Pressing my face against the glass, I turned from the fields and stared down at a terrace directly below me. In the moon's fitful light, I saw something move in the shadows—a child, I thought, but I couldn't be sure. For a better look, I opened the casement and leaned out. As I did so, a cloud covered the moon and threw the terrace into darkness.

When the moon emerged, I saw a cat mincing daintily along the garden wall. Not a child. Just a cat out for a ramble in the dark.

Too cold to stay at the window, I closed the casement and returned to bed.

I woke to a room full of sunshine. Nellie knelt by the hearth, feeding coal to the fire.

Nellie glanced over her shoulder and caught me staring at her. "Beg pardon, miss," she murmured. "I didn't mean to wake ye."

"The sun woke me," I told her, "not you."

She nodded and began gathering her things—a coal scuttle, a scrub brush, and a pail of water.

"You needn't rush off," I said. "Stay awhile."

"Oh, miss, I can't do no such thing. Miss Crutchfield would be cross, very cross indeed. She thinks I'm too slow as it is." By now Nellie was on her feet, headed toward the door. She struggled to manage the bucket and the coal scuttle.

I jumped out of bed and grabbed the bucket just before it slipped from her hand. "You poor thing," I said. "This bucket is much too heavy for you."

"I can manage, miss." Nellie held out her hand for the bucket, but I hid it behind my back.

"First you must tell me about James. What's wrong with him? Is he as sick as Aunt says?"

Nellie busied herself sweeping up soot and a few stray chunks of coal. "Well, miss," she said at last, "there be no doubt Master James is poorly. Ashy white he is, and thin as a bone, fretful as a baby with a bellyache. He sleeps with a light, for the dark scares him. He has fearful bad dreams and wakes up screaming. Dawson don't know what to make of him. It ain't natural, she says, for a boy to carry on like that."

It was the most I'd ever heard Nellie say. Seemingly worn out from talking, she sat down on the hearth stool.

"What was he like before he got sick?" I asked.

"He were sick when I come to the hall. I only been here a few months." She held out her hand. "Can I have me bucket now, miss?"

"Where are you going?"

"To Master James's room, miss."

28

"Wait." After handing her the bucket, I flung on my robe, stepped into my slippers, and followed her down the hall.

"Please, miss." Nellie turned to face me, her eyes filling with tears. "Miss Crutchfield don't allow no one to enter Master James's room without her say-so. She'll have me sacked."

"I just want to see him," I said. "He won't even know I'm there."

Nellie shrugged. "I reckon there be no stopping ye." She turned back, her thin shoulders bent under the weight of the pail and the coal scuttle, and made her way down the hall and past the stairs. On tiptoe, I followed her.

Nellie stopped in front of a closed door and set down her bucket. As she began to turn the knob, the door suddenly swung open. Aunt stood on the threshold, frowning down at poor Nellie, who dropped her brush in fright.

"How often must I tell you to knock before entering a room?" Aunt said to Nellie. "You don't have the sense you were born with—that is, if you were born with any sense at all."

Nellie scurried into James's room before the woman could say any more, and Aunt closed the door.

I made a move to return to my room without being seen, but Aunt spied me. Striding toward me, she grasped my arm. "In proper households, young ladies do not go about in their robes and nightgowns."

"You're hurting me," I protested.

Aunt released me so abruptly, I almost lost my balance. "Dress yourself." With that, she hurried downstairs, her back as straight as a broomstick, her black dress rustling like dry leaves.

Rubbing my arm, I stared at the closed door at the end of the hall. At least I knew where James was.

FOUR

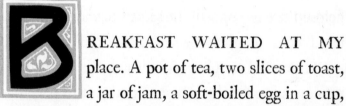

BREAKFAST WAITED AT MY place. A pot of tea, two slices of toast, a jar of jam, a soft-boiled egg in a cup, and two pieces of bacon. A book lay beside my plate—*Pilgrim's Progress* by John Bunyan.

I knew who'd put it there. I also knew that I had no intention of opening it. Once in a desperate search for something to read, I'd tried to interest myself in Pilgrim's journey, but I'd found him an unpleasant hero who'd left his wife and children behind to search for his own salvation. I'd gotten as far as the slough of despond and tossed the book aside, thoroughly bored with both Pilgrim and his progress.

Turning to my meal, I found that my egg was cold, my toast was cold, my tea was cold, and my bacon was more fat than meat. I glanced at the clock ticking solemnly on the sideboard and realized that I was an hour late. Small wonder my food wasn't hot.

After eating what I could, I grabbed my coat and ran outdoors, eager to escape the gloomy house. The wind nipped my cheeks and ears and nose and tangled my hair, but the rain had stopped and the air was fresh and cold. Cloud shadows raced across the fields. Ravens hopped about the terrace and chattered to one another like schoolchildren on holiday.

The cat I'd seen last night was grooming itself in a sunny spot. I did my best to entice it to play, but every time I got within touching distance it would run off again.

I heard someone laugh and wheeled around to see an old man watching me. He wore a tweed jacket, faded corduroy pants patched at the knees, and a red wool scarf knotted round his neck. Despite his bristly beard and pointed nose, he had a kindly look.

"If that don't be a cat fer ye," he said. "Only lets ye pet him if it suits 'im."

"Does he have a name?"

"He be called Cat like all the others afore him. No sense us naming 'em. They got their own names, secret from us'n." He chuckled. "I have a name, though. It be Spratt. Mr. Samuel Spratt. I be gardener, groundskeeper, driver. Whatever Mr. Crutchfield needs me to do, I do."

By now, Cat was perched several feet away on the head of a statue. Tail twitching, he regarded me with disdain.

"Ye'd be better off with a dog," Spratt said. "A dog cares about ye. Might even save yer life. Which no cat would do."

"I've never had a dog," I said. "Or a cat, for that matter."

"Master James had a dog name of Nero. A terrier. Good ratters they be, but not Nero. He were spoiled. Wouldn't dirty his little white paws digging up a rat tunnel."

"What happened to Nero?"

"He were run over by a farm wagon. It near broke Master James's heart. He were right fond of that little dog." Spratt gazed into the distance. Without looking at me, he said, "It were her fault, ye know. Her throwed a ball right in front of that wagon and

Nero gone after it. I swear she done it a-purpose. A spiteful thing, she were."

I stared at the old man, horrified. Surely he couldn't be speaking of Sophia. A girl from the village, maybe. A servant. But not the perfect Sophia. "You must be mistaken," I said. "It was an accident, surely."

Spratt came back to the present with a jolt. "Lord, I be getting old and addled. Don't know what I were talking about, thinking of somewhat else altogether. Happens when ye get old like me. Things run together—time past, time present. Time future, for all's I know."

Taking a moment to gather his wits, he touched the brim of his cap and said, "Ye must be Miss Florence." He smiled at me. "What do a young lady all the way from London think of the country?"

"It's beautiful," I said, still unnerved by his account of Nero's death. "But it's very quiet."

"Most city folks comes here for the quiet," he said.

"I suppose when you're old it must be very calming."

He laughed as if I amused him. Encouraged, I followed him deeper into the garden. While he pruned shrubbery, I told him about the orphanage and my friends there and how big and noisy London was and how long the coach ride had been. He had little to say, so I talked until I ran out of things to tell him. "I think I'll explore the garden now," I finally announced.

Spratt laughed. "Me ears do be in need of a rest, miss." He gave me a clumsy pat on the shoulder, a bit like a trained bear might. "Be careful how ye go. Stay on the path and don't step on nothing. Yer aunt don't like folks in the garden, but I don't see no harm in it."

I set off with some excitement. Heretofore, my jaunts had been limited to outings in Kew Gardens with the other orphans. We'd never been allowed to put one foot off the path. Hand in hand with our partners, we'd strolled slowly behind Miss Medleycoate. No pausing to watch a squirrel or a bird. No flower picking. No talking or laughing.

Forgetting Spratt's warning, I ran and hopped and skipped, turning down one path and then another. I watched two squirrels chase each other up and down and round a tree. When they saw me, they chattered as if they were scolding me for spying on them.

After about half an hour, I thought I heard someone following me. I looked this way and that but saw no one. The wind sighed in the bare branches of a tall oak. Birds hopped about in the bushes. A rabbit darted across my path and vanished into the shrubbery. Was that what I'd heard? Ordinary outdoor noises?

I walked a little farther. My skin prickled again. Someone was nearby, I was sure of it this time— someone watching me from the hedges and shrubs.

I turned quickly and began running back the way I'd come, but instead of reaching the house, I found myself beside a pool I didn't remember passing. In its center was a fountain topped with a statue of a boy and a girl holding a swan. Tiers of thick icicles dripped from the swan's beak.

An inscription had been carved into the fountain's stone rim. I bent down to make out the time-worn words.

Here and There and Everywhere.

"Here and there and everywhere," I whispered. "Here and there and everywhere."

Certain it was a riddle, I touched each letter, tracing the curves and angles, but I couldn't come up with the answer.

Surrounded by a dense growth of tall yews, the clearing was a forbidding place. Dark clouds blew across the sun, and I shivered, suddenly cold. I was hungry, too. Time to go back to the house, I thought. But where was it?

Four paths led away from the pool, laid out like spokes in a wheel. I looked behind me at the way I'd come, then at the other paths, but I didn't know which one to choose. I'd run this way and that through the garden, paying no mind to directions.

Finally I chose a path at random and began walking quickly, then running. After ten minutes, I found myself at the pool again. Breathless with fright, I chose another path with the same result. Desperate, I tried the last path and once more found myself staring at the fountain. It seemed I couldn't escape from those two stone children and their captive swan.

Suddenly laughter broke out again, loud and shrill, a child's laugh.

I spun around, expecting to see Nellie. I saw no one, but the shrubbery shook as if someone hid there. "You can't scare me," I cried, more angry now than frightened. "Come out and face me, Nellie!"

The shrubbery rustled. "Hide and seek," a voice called. "You're it!"

Pushing aside a yew's heavy branches, I ran after the voice. The trees' needles whipped against my face, caught my hair, snagged my coat. I tripped on knotted roots and fell more than once. Sometimes the laughter was ahead of me, sometimes behind, but each time I thought I was close, my tormentor eluded me, laughing all the while.

In tears, I burst out of the yews and saw the house at last. "No more games, Nellie," I called. "Where are you?"

"Come and find me," the voice cried from somewhere in the yews. "If you dare!"

"You can't fool me, Nellie! Come out at once!"

Nellie didn't answer. Nor did she appear. The yews swayed softly in the wind, but nothing else moved.

"I'm not leaving until you come out!" I waited on the terrace until my feet hurt from the cold, but Nellie stayed hidden. At last I gave up and ran inside.

Mrs. Dawson looked up from the pot she was stirring. "Miss Florence," she said. "Where have you been? It's almost time for tea."

Before I had a chance to answer, she looked at me closely. "Your face is scratched—you're bleeding."

"It's Nellie's fault," I said. "I got lost chasing her in the garden, but I never did find her."

Mrs. Dawson stared at me as if I'd spoken in Chinese. "Nellie's got no time for games. She's been inside working the whole time you've been outside."

I stared at Mrs. Dawson. "If it wasn't Nellie, who was it?"

"I have no idea what you're talking about." Mrs. Dawson examined my cuts and scratches. "These need tending to before they get infected."

Suddenly tired, I sank down in a chair and let Mrs. Dawson wash my face. She worked deftly and gently and took time to comb the tangles from my hair.

"Let me tell you something," she said. "Neither your uncle nor your aunt wants to hear stories about children you may or may not have seen in the garden."

"But—"

Mrs. Dawson took my chin in her hand and looked me in the eye. "You heard me, miss. Keep that talk to yourself."

I watched her cross the room and open the oven door. Out came the smell of fresh-baked bread. "Would you like some?" she asked.

"Oh, yes, please."

Mrs. Dawson sliced off the end of a loaf, spread it with butter, and handed it to me. "No more stories."

I bit into the bread, the best I'd ever tasted. "I don't understand—"

"That's just it, miss. You're new to this place. There's much you don't know and even more you don't understand. So listen to them that's been here longer than you, and hush."

"But—"

"Finish that bread and go find someone else to pester." Cross now, Mrs. Dawson began chopping onions with a knife that could have cut off my head.

Frustrated and confused, I ate my bread in silence. Someone had teased me in the garden. If Mrs. Dawson was right, it could not have been Nellie.

I hesitated in the doorway. Mrs. Dawson glanced at me. "Well, what is it now?" she asked, still cross.

"Do children from the village ever play in the garden?"

Mrs. Dawson mulled that over. "Of course," she said. "That's what you heard. One of those naughty rascals was teasing you." She smiled then, her anger forgotten. "Don't tell anyone you saw them. Miss Crutchfield would order Spratt to chase them away."

I went to my room, glad the mystery was solved. If I heard the children again, I'd find them this time, and become their friend.

FIVE

ॐ

THE NEXT DAY, IT RAINED. THE day after that, it rained again. By the fourth day of unrelenting rain, I was tired of reading, tired of sketching, and tired of myself. I missed the girls at the orphanage and devoted hours to writing to each of them, describing in detail my tedious life at Crutchfield Hall.

I wrote to Miss Beatty, as well, but not to Miss Medleycoate, who would most likely answer with a long letter reprimanding me for being an ungrateful girl who complained when fortune smiled upon her.

It occurred to me that I was indeed ungrateful. Compared to what I'd endured at Miss Medleycoate's establishment, I had nothing to complain of.

I had no chores, I had books to read, I never went to bed hungry. A little boredom was nothing to complain about.

Thrusting my letters into the fire, I watched them burn. Later I'd try writing again to my former companions, but feared it might be a difficult task. If I didn't complain, they might think I was bragging. If I complained, they might think I had forgotten what I'd escaped by leaving the orphanage.

I'd finished *Great Expectations* the night before, so I decided to go downstairs and look for something else to read.

After some thought, I selected *Vanity Fair* from the shelves in the sitting room. I'd heard Becky Sharp was a wicked girl, and I thought I'd enjoy reading about someone worse than myself.

On my way to the stairs, I passed my uncle's study. The door was open, and I decided to have a look. His books were dull, having to do with law and history and collections of essays by men such as Carlyle and Macaulay. His papers consisted of deeds and other legal matters, some of them quite old and brittle and written in Latin.

Uncle had a large globe on a stand. I spun it round and round and stopped it with my finger. I pretended to be in the place my finger landed. First I was lost at sea in the Pacific Ocean, a female Robinson Crusoe in search of a desert island. Then it was on to Africa, where I explored jungles and escaped from lions. In America, I traveled in a stage-coach pursued by Indians. At the North Pole, I nearly perished in the cold but was rescued by Eskimos.

Tiring of that, I made up stories about the por-traits hanging on the walls—long-nosed ladies with small chins and close-set eyes, red-faced gentlemen with round cheeks and bushy whiskers, handsome young men with curly hair and dimples in their chins, pretty girls with rosy lips and cheeks. I imag-ined them riding horses and dancing at balls, falling in love, marrying, living to be old or dying tragi-cally young.

I had no idea who the subjects actually were or what had become of them, or even if they were my ancestors or someone else's. All I knew was that they'd been painted long ago.

When I'd run out of stories, I examined the things on my uncle's desk. I nearly cut myself on a fancy letter opener. I spun a revolving stand filled with pipes of many shapes and sizes. I examined the pictures on tobacco tins. And then I spotted an oval photograph of a boy and a girl.

Judging by the style of their clothes, the children could have been photographed yesterday. The girl was about my age and very pretty. Her hair was long and dark and curly like mine, tied back with a ribbon the same way I wore mine. The boy was several years younger, about nine, I guessed. His hair was a mop of dark curls, but his face was rounder than the girl's and his expression sweeter. Sophia and James, I thought. They had to be.

To get a better look, I took the picture to the window. Sophia had my straight nose and oval face, but she had Aunt's narrow-lipped mouth, and the expression on her face was sulky. She stood stiffly, as if she didn't want to be closer than necessary to her brother.

My musing was interrupted by Aunt's voice. "What are you doing in here? You have no business touching the things on your uncle's desk. Put that down!"

I was so startled, I dropped the photograph. The glass in the frame broke with a sharp snap. As I stooped to pick it up, I pricked my finger on a sliver. Horrified, I watched a drop of my blood fall on Sophia's face.

Aunt snatched the picture. "Look what you've done! The photograph is ruined."

"I'm sorry, Aunt." As I spoke, I wrapped my handkerchief around my finger to stop the bleeding. "I didn't mean—"

With an angry look, she interrupted me. "Your uncle will be quite upset when he sees this. I will speak to him as soon as he returns from town." Photograph in hand, my aunt wheeled about to leave the study.

I hurried after her. "Please, Aunt," I cried. "I'm sorry, truly sorry."

"Go to your room," she said. "And do not come down for supper. Nellie will bring your meals."

"But, Aunt—"

She turned a cold and angry face to me. "Go to your room immediately—or I shall see that you stay there until I find a suitable boarding school for you."

Left alone in the room, I listened to my aunt's footsteps fade away. I'd wanted to ask her if the girl was Sophia, if the boy was James, but she'd given me no opportunity. As usual, I'd offended her.

Worse yet, she'd threatened to send me to boarding school. Despite my aunt's unkindness, I did not want to leave Crutchfield Hall. Boarding school might be no better than Miss Medleycoate's establishment.

Evening was coming on fast. In the silence, the room grew colder and darker. A draft stirred the air around me, and for a moment I felt something like the touch of a cold hand on my cheek. Certain that I was being watched, I moved closer to the fire.

When Nellie brought my supper, I was still huddled by the hearth, brooding on Aunt's conduct toward me.

"I'm sorry Miss Crutchfield were so angry with you," Nellie said. "She have a wicked temper. I sees it meself when I do wrong."

"It's not just her temper, Nellie. She hates me."

Nellie fidgeted with her apron. She seemed to want to tell me something but wasn't sure she should. Finally she said, "Ye mustn't ever tell Dawson this, but her says it's account of Miss Sophia that yer aunt hates ye so. Yer aunt thinks Mr. Crutchfield brung ye here to take Miss Sophia's place. And her don't want ye, her wants Miss Sophia. Nobody else. Just her."

"But Nellie, how can that be? Sophia is dead. Aunt can't bring her back."

"Dawson says Miss Crutchfield be daft." Nellie tapped the side of her head.

I didn't know what to say. I was so accustomed to Miss Medleycoate's behavior, I'd assumed Aunt was of a similar disposition. Mean spirited and cross, but not crazy.

"It's on account of Miss Sophia that there be so few servants," Nellie went on. "Folk from the village are scared to work here. Some even say Crutchfield Hall be haunted." Here Nellie's eyes widened, and her voice dropped. "Do ye ever feel someone a-watching ye?"

"Sometimes." The room was quiet, hushed.

"They say it be Miss Sophia," Nellie whispered. "They say her won't lie quiet in her grave."

Suddenly Nellie hid her head under her apron like a child hiding under the blankets. "Oh, lord, I be a-scaring meself," she cried. "I can't bear thinking on spirits, miss. It's only the wicked what comes back. The good stays in the ground and waits for the Lord's call on Judgment Day."

Equally scared, I patted Nellie's shaking shoulders. I'd never given much thought to ghosts before.

Just getting through each day at the orphanage had taken all my energy. But now, in this dark house, with time to spare, the spirit world seemed very real. Maybe even dangerous.

At last, Nellie emerged from her apron, her face blotchy with tears. "Oh, miss, I pray there be no ghosts here." With that, she jumped up and headed for the door. "Dawson must be a-wondering where I'm at. There be work to do afore I goes to bed."

No longer hungry for my supper, I went upstairs to my room. There I undressed quickly and climbed into bed. With the covers snug around me, I felt warmer and safer. I planned to read *Vanity Fair* until I was too sleepy to make sense of the story, and then I'd go to sleep.

Just as I'd gotten comfortable, I heard a knock on my door. It was Uncle, come to say good night.

"I hear my sister was quite cross with you this afternoon," he said.

"Yes." I bit my thumbnail and looked at him sadly. "I'm very sorry I broke the glass on the frame, Uncle. I hope I didn't ruin the photograph."

"Don't worry, Florence. The picture is fine. All it needs is a new piece of glass." He reached for my hand and looked at my finger. "Did you wash the cut?"

"Yes, Uncle. It was just a nick."

He hesitated, taking a moment to smooth my blankets and adjust the lamp's wick, before he crossed the room to the fireplace. "The picture was taken almost a year ago, shortly before Sophia died."

I sat up straight and stared at Uncle. "How did she die?"

He stirred the fire with a poker. The blue flames leapt a little higher and made shadows dance on the wall. "Sophia had a bad fall," he said in a low voice. "She and James were playing together when it happened."

Giving the fire another poke, Uncle said, "Sometimes I fear the boy wants nothing more than to die himself. It's as if he believes his death will atone for hers."

We sat together and watched the fire. The wind tugged and pried at the windows, making the curtains sway.

After a while, Uncle got to his feet. As he leaned down to kiss me good night, I found the nerve to ask him one last question. "What was Sophia like?"

"Sophia." Uncle spoke her name as if it were a long, soft sigh, a winter wind in the treetops, a drift of snow, a wash of water over stones. "It's hard to say what Sophia was like. She was a difficult child, quick to anger and long to sulk. She was quiet and secretive, not always truthful, and often unkind to James."

I looked at Uncle, puzzled. "But Aunt adored her."

"Yes, she spoiled her with pretty dresses and dolls. Never scolded her, never found fault, never made her behave. Unfortunately, Sophia did not return her aunt's affection. Indeed, she took advantage of my sister."

I seized Uncle's hand. "Do you believe in ghosts?"

"No, indeed." He chuckled. "Why do you ask?"

"People in the village think Crutchfield Hall is haunted. Did you know that?"

Uncle laughed. "The villagers are a superstitious lot. Pay their stories no heed, Florence." He looked at me closely. "You're not frightened, are you?"

"Sometimes I think Sophia is still here," I said quietly. "I feel her following me, watching me, listening to me. Wherever I go, she's nearby."

Uncle looked at me earnestly, his kind face filled with concern. "Oh, my dear, foolish child, that's quite impossible. When we die, we leave this world and do not return. Be a sensible girl." He handed me

Vanity Fair. "Read your Thackeray. You'll find no ghosts in his stories, just ordinary people like you and me and a thousand others going about the world as we must."

Uncle sat with me for a while, trying to calm me. I was too imaginative, I was too sensitive, I was alone too much, he said. Because I wanted to please him, I did my best to dismiss my fears as silly and childish.

After he left, I listened to his footsteps until I heard them no more. Let Uncle believe what he liked, but I knew Sophia was here in this house. I hadn't imagined the laughter and the voice in the garden, or that cold hand on my cheek. Sophia was watching me, and I didn't know if I should fear her or try to befriend her.

SIX

THE NEXT DAY I WOKE ONCE more to the sound of rain driven hard against my window. I dressed and went down to breakfast, deliberately arriving too late to join Aunt or Uncle. I was not in a happy mood. I'd slept poorly, waking from one bad dream after another. Sophia traipsed through each one, taunting me, chasing me, frightening me. Sometimes she looked like a living girl, but in the worst dreams, her face was a skull and her bony hands stretched toward me like claws.

When I'd eaten all I could, which wasn't very much, I wandered through the house aimlessly, drifting from room to room, lonely, sad, and scared. Uncle had gone to Lewes on business, and Aunt had gone with him. James was shut up in his room, too sick to be a companion. Nellie was hard at work somewhere in the house, and Mrs. Dawson was busy in the kitchen. Neither had time for me.

But I wasn't alone. No matter where I was, no matter whether it was day or night, Sophia hovered in the shadows, watching and listening, daring me to find her.

I climbed the stairs to the second floor, but instead of going to my room, I went to James's room and stood at his door. All was quiet within. What did he do all day? How long could books interest him if he did nothing but read? I was tempted to turn the knob and confront him.

But I didn't do it. Aunt would find out. She'd already threatened to send me away to boarding school. If I flagrantly disobeyed her, she'd make sure I went as soon as possible.

I backed away from James's room. What else was there to do? I was tired of reading, tired of drawing, tired of being trapped inside by the rain and the wind.

At the bottom of the stairs to the third floor, I paused. Aunt had told me there was nothing up there but empty rooms where the servants used to live. Maybe she was right, but exploring those rooms would give me something new to do.

At the top, I was confronted by a narrow hall lined with closed doors. I opened one after another. Except for dust, spider webs, and more dust, the small rooms were all empty. Curtainless windows looked out on bare fields under dark clouds and pouring rain.

I found a dead bird in one room, most likely trapped inside last summer. I touched its brittle feathers lightly, then drew back. Its dark, dull eyes frightened me.

At the end of the hall, I stopped in front of the last closed door. I struggled to turn the knob, but it wouldn't move. To get a better grip, I wrapped my skirt around the knob and used all my strength. At last it yielded, and I shoved the door open. In front of me, a narrow flight of stairs led up to the dark attic.

Over my head, the wind rumbled. Rain beat against the roof. I heard creaking sounds and rustlings. I thought of Jane Eyre's climb to the tower where Mr. Rochester kept his insane wife. Things worse than a dead bird could be up there.

As I hesitated, I heard the cleaning woman's voice on the floor below. I'd forgotten it was her day to come. My fear of being discovered was greater than my fear of the attic's secrets. As quietly as possible, I closed the door behind me, plunging myself into a cold darkness given voice by the wind and the rain.

Cautiously, I climbed the creaking steps, listening for odd sounds and watching for signs of danger.

Dim light leaked in through a row of small windows under the eaves. Gradually furniture emerged from the shadows—bureaus, chairs, mirrors, boxes and chests, heaps of old, mildewed books. I opened drawers and cabinets crammed with faded silks, ancient linens, and yellowing documents written in Latin. I peered into boxes and found tarnished silverware, chipped bowls, cracked plates, and dainty cups without handles.

In hope of finding something more interesting, I looked around and spied a large trunk. Lifting its curved lid, I was amazed to find myself staring into the faces of half a dozen dolls. They had long curly hair and rosy cheeks. Their hands and feet were delicate. Their dresses were silk. They looked brand new, untouched, sleeping as if nothing would ever wake them.

Gently, I lifted one out. Her hair was dark and curly, and her eyes were the same blue as her dress. Her lips were parted in a smile revealing tiny white teeth and the tip of a pink tongue. She wore white stockings and button-top shoes.

In the orphanage, we used to daydream about dolls like these. We saw them in shops when we went out for walks with Miss Beatty. While she waited patiently, we pressed our noses against the window and chose our favorites, the ones we'd buy if we were rich. I always called mine Clara Annette, a beautiful name, I thought.

This doll, I thought, would be my Clara Annette. I had no idea who she belonged to or why she was in the attic. I did not care. I'd found her and I planned to keep her. In the daytime, I'd hide her in my wardrobe under the spare blankets and quilts. In the nighttime, she'd sleep with me.

Laying Clara Annette gently on a nearby chair, I moved the other dolls aside to see what else was in the trunk. Wrapped in tissue paper were dresses and slips, nightgowns and robes, coats and hats, shoes and stockings and underwear. I held up a blue silk dress and stared at myself in an age specked mirror. It had been made for a girl about my size. Like the doll's dress, the dress matched my eyes.

As I turned this way and that, admiring my reflection, I felt a familiar shiver run up my spine. Clasping the dress to my chest, I stared about me. "Is that you, Sophia?" I whispered to the shadows.

Rain pounded on the roof and gales of winter wind moaned in the eaves. But no one answered.

"Why do you hide from me?" I called.

I heard a rustling sound, followed by a giggle. "It's a game," Sophia whispered. "I found you—now you must find me."

Dropping the dress, I ran toward Sophia's voice. "Where are you?"

"Here, there, everywhere," she whispered, repeating the fountain's riddle. "Here, there, everywhere."

I whirled in circles, trying to locate her, but I couldn't. She truly was here, there, and everywhere. Suddenly frightened, I said, "Go away. Leave me alone."

"Don't you want me to be your friend?" She came closer, so close I could feel her cold breath on my cheek. "Aren't you lonely, Florence?"

"How can you be my friend? I can't see you, I don't know where you are."

"You're afraid of me," Sophia said scornfully.

"Yes," I cried, "yes, I am. I'm afraid of you! You, you—"

"Why don't you say it?" Sophia mocked me. "I'm dead. That's why you're afraid."

The cold air came closer, circled me once or twice, and then backed away. "How can I harm you? I have no substance. No strength."

With a whisper of silk, the dress I'd dropped slid across the floor toward me as if blown by the wind. I jumped back when it touched my shoes.

"Take it," Sophia whispered. "You need a new dress. That drab rag is dreadful. It's the sort of thing a pauper orphan would wear to scrub the floor."

I looked at the silk dress, fearful of it yet wanting it.

"If Aunt loved you as she loved me, she'd lavish expensive gowns on you as she did me." Sophia sighed. "Judging by what I've seen, I'm certain she doesn't even like you. Indeed, I believe she despises you."

Head down, I gazed at the dress. I couldn't argue with the truth.

"She hates you because you're not me," Sophia added.

I remained silent.

"Aunt gave me everything in that trunk," Sophia said. "After I died, I watched her pack my dresses and dolls as if she thought I'd come back for them someday." She laughed. "Poor old Aunt. She wept as if her heart were broken."

As Sophia spoke, Clara Annette floated across the attic and dropped softly into my arms. Without intending to, I hugged the doll. She was too beautiful to leave in the attic.

"I can't take your things," I whispered, holding the doll even tighter.

"Of course you can," Sophia said. "I want you to have them as a token of our friendship. Besides, I have no need for dresses or dolls now."

"Aunt will not want me to have them."

"Tut," Sophia said with a laugh. "Aunt needn't know."

I stared into the shadows and tried to see her. But no matter how hard I looked, I saw nothing. "Please, Sophia," I begged. "Please let me see you."

"Someday." With that promise, a cold breeze whirled away, taking Sophia with it.

Scooping up the dress and the doll, I ran down the attic steps, mindless now of how much noise I made. Behind me, the door to the attic slammed shut.

In my room, safe behind my own door, I dropped the dress on my bed. With Clara Annette in my arms, I warmed myself in front of the fire. Why had I accepted Sophia's gifts? I didn't want the belongings of a dead girl. Yet I'd been unable to refuse them. Because they were beautiful, I supposed. Because I'd never owned anything like them. Because I was afraid of angering Sophia.

A soft rap on my door startled me. Clutching the doll even tighter, I cried, "Who's there?"

"It's Nellie, miss, come to tidy your room." The door opened a crack and Nellie peered in. Never was I so happy to see her ordinary freckled face.

Nellie stared at the dress on the bed and the doll in my arms. "Oh, miss," she whispered, entering the room, "they be ever so pretty. Did your uncle give you them?" As she spoke, she touched the silk gently.

I shook my head. It was then that Nellie noticed my state. "Why, miss, what be wrong?"

"No one gave them to me. I found them in the attic."

"Ye went to the attic?" The sympathy on Nellie's

face changed to shock. "Nobody goes there. The floor be rotten. Even a body small as me could fall through."

From the corner behind me I heard a soft sound. The rustling of a dress maybe. A sigh, a laugh so low, I wasn't sure I really heard it. Sophia was there, watching me, assessing me, scorning me, scorning Nellie.

Despite myself, I was beginning to feel cross. "Do you always do what people tell you to do, Nellie? Don't you have any curiosity?"

"I knows my place, miss," Nellie said in an annoyingly humble voice.

I was horrified to find myself wanting to slap her face or pull her hair. It was what Sophia would have done.

"I know it ain't right for me to tell ye what to do, but don't go up there again," Nellie begged. "And don't keep them pretty things. They ain't yers."

While Nellie talked, Sophia whispered, "Don't listen to her. She's an ignorant servant. Keep the doll, keep the dress. She's jealous because I gave them to you instead of to her."

"No," I heard myself say to Nellie, "it's not right for a stupid girl like you to tell *me* what to do. Go back to the kitchen where you belong. I'm tired of your foolish chatter."

"Oh, miss." Nellie gave me a horrified look and ran from my room.

As soon as she was gone, I wanted to call her back. What was wrong with me? I'd never spoken to anyone like that, and I was ashamed of myself. I'd been cruel, thoughtlessly and needlessly cruel.

At the same time, I was aware of Sophia watching me from the shadows. Had she put those words into my mouth? Was it she who made me speak so cruelly to poor little Nellie?

I knew that Sophia would scorn me if I ran after Nellie. No one apologized to a servant. It simply wasn't done.

So I stayed where I was and stroked Clara Annette's dark ringlets. "Such a pretty doll," I whispered. "Do you miss your old owner?"

"Of course she misses me," Sophia said. "Everybody misses me. I was the favorite—until James came along and ruined everything."

On noiseless feet, a shadowy shape crept toward me. The closer it came, the colder I was. It was as if winter had taken a form and entered my warm room.

At first, Sophia was no more distinct than a figure glimpsed through fog or mist, but as she came nearer, her wavering outline slowly solidified. She wore a stained white silk dress, and her dainty slippers were muddy. What was left of her dark hair was dull and sparse. Her face was narrow and pale, her skin stretched tightly over her skull. Dark shadows ringed her eyes. Her teeth were brown. She smelled of earth and mold.

In abhorrence, I closed my eyes and tried to tell her to leave, but my mouth shook so badly, I couldn't speak. Never had I seen such a dreadful sight.

"Look at me," Sophia said.

Unwillingly, I opened my eyes. "What do you want with me?" I whispered.

"I'm so cold and so lonely." Sophia nestled into the rocking chair beside me, as weightless as a puff of cold air. "I need a friend, and so do you. We could be like sisters, sharing secrets."

I studied her white face, her stained teeth, her unruly hair, her dull eyes. "I don't want to be your friend. Or your sister. I won't, I can't." To my shame, I began to cry.

Sophia gave me a narrow-lipped smile, just the

sort I'd expect to see on my aunt's face. "I tell you, you *will* be my friend, whether you wish to be or not. I always get my way. It's useless to fight me."

With that, she slipped out of the chair and disappeared as quickly as she'd come. For a moment the coal fire flared up; then it died down to embers.

In shock, I gazed at the place where Sophia had first materialized. She'd stood right there beside the bed. She'd squeezed into the chair beside me, close enough for me to smell her. She'd spoken to me.

Uncle said the dead did not return. He was wrong.

Unable to stop shaking, I stared at Clara Annette's china face. Sophia's doll, I reminded myself. Not mine.

Filled with revulsion, I threw the doll across the room. Her head hit the edge of the mantel and she landed on the floor. Like a child fatally injured in a bad fall, she sprawled on her back, arms flung out, head broken.

Stricken to see such a pretty thing ruined, I picked her up and hid her in the back of a drawer full of extra linens. It wouldn't do for Aunt to see her gift to Sophia so badly treated.

Stricken to see such a pretty thing ruined, I picked her up and hid her in the back of a drawer full of extra linens. It wouldn't do for Aunt to see her gift to Sophia so badly treated.

Not daring to leave the dress on the bed, I scooped it up and stuffed it into the wardrobe, behind my best dress and my coat.

Once dress and doll were hidden, I ran downstairs. I did not want to remain alone in my room for fear Sophia might return.

SEVEN

NCLE AND AUNT HAD NOT
come back from their trip to town, so I
joined Mrs. Dawson in the kitchen. To
my relief, Nellie wasn't there. After speaking to her
so rudely, I couldn't face her.

"You look poorly," Mrs. Dawson said. "Are you
coming down with something?"

I shook my head. "I'm just tired."

"Drink your tea. It should perk you up."

I poured milk into my cup, added sugar, and filled
it with tea. Steam rose around my face, comforting
me. I breathed in the sweet smell of Earl Grey, my
favorite blend, rich with bergamot.

Mrs. Dawson sliced bread and passed it over to me, along with a serving of shepherd's pie. Its mashed-potato crust was baked golden, and the vegetables and beef inside filled the kitchen with an aroma that made me hungry in spite of myself.

Mrs. Dawson watched me eat. "You may not be ailing," she said, "but something's eating at you."

Looking Mrs. Dawson in the eye, I said, "Do you believe in ghosts?"

Mrs. Dawson must have heard the fear in my voice. Studying me closely, she said, "Has something frightened you, Florence?"

Surrendering to my need for comfort, I flung my arms around her and pressed my face against her soft body. "Sophia," I sobbed. "I saw her today. She was hideous, horrible, monstrous."

Mrs. Dawson rocked me gently. "No, no, Florence. Sophia is dead and gone."

"But I tell you, I saw her," I insisted. "She *spoke* to me."

Mrs. Dawson took me by my shoulders and held me at arm's length. "And I tell you, you dreamed it." Her eyes implored me to agree with her. "You're lonely here, you want a friend, and you've made yourself believe in Sophia."

I shook my head. "Surely Aunt has seen her—"

"No more, no more. I'll hear no more." Mrs. Dawson's voice quivered as if I was scaring her. "The poor child's soul rests in peace now. Father Browne saw to it. He blessed her proper."

Making a shooing motion, she said, "Go on now. Find a book to read. Forget the dream. Forget Sophia. Say nothing about her to Nellie or anyone else. You'll only bring grief on yourself."

Defeated, I gave up and left Mrs. Dawson to her work. As I walked away, I heard laughter in the shadows. A cold finger brushed my cheek. Footsteps pattered behind me. I did not look back. I knew who it was.

At the top of the steps, Sophia appeared beside me, her face tinged blue, her eyes circled with dark smudges like bruises. "Why don't you visit James?" she whispered. "I know you want to."

I drew back, repulsed by the smell of damp earth that clung to her. "Aunt and Uncle forbid it."

"I never let others stop *me* from doing what I want." Keeping her hand on my arm, she floated into my room as if no more than air, but I could not break away from her.

My wardrobe opened, and Sophia pulled out the

blue silk dress. "Wear this. You must be presentable if you are to visit James."

Even though I knew it was futile to argue, I said, "I am not going to visit James." But as I spoke, I found myself taking off my own drab brown dress and slipping into the blue silk. The fabric touched my skin, as delicate as butterfly wings.

Sophia picked up my brush and comb and began brushing my hair. When it shone as brown and glossy as hers once did, she tied it back with a blue velvet ribbon. "There," she said. "You're not nearly as pretty as I am, but I suppose you'll do."

I wanted to tell her she was not pretty now, but instead I stood silently before the mirror and admired my reflection. Instead of a wretched orphan, I saw a well-dressed girl, the sort I'd admired on the streets of London.

Behind me, I noticed Sophia kept her back to the mirror. "Why don't you stand beside me and look at yourself? Then you can see who's prettier—you or me." It was a terrible thing to say, and I was ashamed of myself for speaking the words out loud.

Ignoring my question, Sophia seized my hand and led me away from the mirror and out of my room. As we walked down the hall, the blue silk rustled like autumn leaves. My hair was a soft, sweet weight on my shoulders and neck. I walked lightly, gracefully. I forgot to be afraid, forgot to worry. At last I was going to meet my cousin James.

Sophia stopped in front of James's door. First she pressed her ear to the wood and listened. Then she bent to peek through the keyhole.

Straightening, she favored me with her thin-lipped smile. "He's all alone, sitting in bed, reading. Don't bother to knock. Just walk in and stand quietly until he notices you. He loves surprises."

"Aren't you coming with me?" I asked.

But I was speaking to empty air. Sophia was gone, leaving an echo of her laughter behind.

For a moment, I hesitated. Perhaps it was unwise to enter without knocking. Suppose I frightened James? What if Sophia was tricking me into doing something I shouldn't? Could I trust her to be truthful?

But I simply could not resist visiting my cousin. Quietly I turned the knob and slowly opened the door. The curtains were closed tightly, and the fire burned low. An oil lamp beside the bed gave enough light for me to see James. Propped up on pillows, he was deeply engrossed in a book.

Like Sophia, he bore little resemblance to the child in the photograph. His round cheeks were gone, leaving his face narrow and solemn. His skin was pale, and the hair tumbling over his eyes was long and curly. Even from this distance, I could see he was thin and frail. Sickly.

Cautiously I took a few steps forward, unsure whether I should approach him or tiptoe out of his room. What I was doing seemed intrusive, rather as if I'd entered a sanctuary without permission.

I must have made a sound, for suddenly he turned and saw me. His reaction horrified me.

"No," he screamed, "you can't cross my threshold. It's forbidden! Get out! Get out!" He was on his knees now, hurling a book at me. Then another and another.

The heavy volumes hit the wall over my head, and I ducked this way and that to avoid being struck. He was definitely stronger than he looked.

When he ran out of books to throw, James fell back against his pillow, shrieking and crying. "Don't come near me!"

I ran to him and seized his hands. "Don't be afraid. I'm Florence, your cousin. Hasn't Uncle told you about me?"

"You can't trick me," James cried. "I know who you are—I know what you want!"

"No, no, James, please listen. I'm Florence Crutchfield. My father was your father's brother. I'm an orphan, just as you are. We're both wards of our uncle, Thomas Crutchfield."

Gradually, James's struggles lessened, and I released his hands. Although he still trembled, he breathed more naturally and his body began to relax.

He studied my face. "You're not Sophia," he whispered, "but you're wearing her dress and your hair is like hers. When I saw you in the shadows by the door, I was certain . . ."

He lay back against the pillows, his face as white as the sheets tumbled about him. "You frightened me."

"I'm so very, very sorry. I didn't mean to, but Sophia—"

"Do you see her too?" he interrupted, his eyes wide with surprise. "I thought I was the only one."

"She made me wear her dress, she fixed my hair, she sent me here . . ." I clenched my fists in vexation. "Please forgive me, James. She, she . . ."

I looked warily around the room. Was Sophia hiding in the corner by the wardrobe? Was she watching from behind the curtains?

James looked at me. "You're afraid of her too."

"She terrifies me. She could be here, she could be there, she could be anywhere."

James took my hands in his small ones. "Not here. We're safe in my room," he said. "She can't cross the threshold."

"Everywhere I go, she goes. The house, the garden. I can't get away from her." I shuddered and continued to search the corners for signs of Sophia.

James shook his head. "Spratt made a charm and hid it over my door. As long as it's there, she can't come in."

"Spratt made a charm?" I stared at my cousin, thinking I'd misunderstood him. "What sort of a charm?"

"Since you come from London," James said, "I doubt you believe in potions and charms and such, but Spratt's mother was a healer. And so was her mother and her mother before her and so on, back and back in time. She taught Spratt all she knew, including the making of charms to ward off evil."

Not sure what I believed, I looked at him, huddled under blankets and propped up on pillows,

trusting in a charm to protect him from his own sister. His dead sister.

I moved nearer to him, fearful of the shadows
around us. "What can Sophia actually do to harm
you? We *see* her, we *hear* her, but she doesn't have a
real body."

Fixing me with the same blue eyes we all had,
James sat up straight and leaned closer to me. "Sophia
doesn't need to be flesh and blood. Haven't you felt the
cold touch of her hand? Hasn't she influenced you?"
He paused and added, "Was it your idea to come to my
room? Did you want to do it, or did she make you?"

My silence answered for me.

James lay back against his pillow, but he kept his
eyes on me. "My sister has no body. She's never hungry. She's never tired. She's never sick. She's free to
concentrate all her energy on one thing and one
thing only. It's all she wants, and she's determined to
have it."

He closed his eyes for a moment as if talking about Sophia's strength had exhausted his own.
The room was so silent, the very air seemed to hold
its breath.

"What does she want?" I whispered.

James looked at me then, his face as pale as the pillow. "She wants me to die." His voice was flat and dull, his eyes almost as lifeless as Sophia's.

"She can't hate you that much. It's unnatural, it's wicked, it's—"

"You don't understand." James's voice rose until he was almost shouting. "It's my fault she's dead. I killed her. I didn't mean to, but I did. And now she wants to kill me."

"How could you have killed her?" I asked. "You're younger and smaller than she is. You—"

"I don't want to talk any more," James cried. "I'm tired and need to rest—you've overexcited me. Go away!"

Confused by the change in his behavior, I reached out to comfort him, but he swung at me, striking me with his fists, not caring whether he hurt me or not. "Go away, I tell you," he shrieked. "Go away!"

Afraid of making him truly ill, I shrank back from the bed. At that moment, the door opened and Aunt entered the room.

At the sight of me, her face lit with joy. Holding out her arms to embrace me, she cried, "You've come back to me! I knew you would. I've saved all your things. I've waited and prayed for your return."

When I recoiled from her touch, Aunt realized her mistake. Immediately her happiness turned to rage. Seizing my shoulders, she shook me so hard, my head bobbled on my neck like a rag doll's. "Where did you get that dress? It's Sophia's, not yours. You have no right to help yourself to her things."

James cowered in his bed, his anger at me forgotten. "Stop, Aunt—you're upsetting me. Do you want me to die too?"

Pushing me aside, Aunt ran to him. "My poor lamb. What has Florence done to you?"

She reached for his hands, but he pushed her away. "Leave me alone! Florence has done nothing to me."

Aunt drew back, rigid with anger. "How dare you speak to me like that! After all I've done for you! Have you no gratitude?"

"Can't you ever leave me alone?" James cried. "I hate you! You wish I'd died instead of her. I heard you say so when you thought I was sleeping."

Unable to bear any more, I ran out of the room. The things I'd imagined in my days at Miss Medleycoate's mocked me. Sisters and brothers were jealous and hateful; they didn't love one another as I'd thought. Aunt was mean and spiteful. Sophia had despised her little brother. James claimed he'd killed his own sister.

After locking myself in my room, I stripped off the blue silk dress, ripping a sleeve in my haste. Buttons popped off and rolled across the floor. Without pausing to think about what I was doing, I stuffed Sophia's dress into the fire.

It smoldered for a moment and then burst into flame. Fire shot up the chimney. Seizing a poker, I did my best to keep it contained. As unhappy as I was, I had no desire to burn Crutchfield Hall to the ground.

With relief, I watched the fire subside. The smoke made my eyes water, and the room reeked of burnt silk. Wearing only a thin slip, I ran to the window and let in a torrent of cold fresh air.

As the casement swung outward, I saw that the constant rain had turned to snow. Trees and shrubbery, roofs and walkways, everything blended together in a sparkling white. Sharp lines disappeared, square shapes softened, hills and flat land merged.

If I'd been in a happier frame of mind, I might have thrilled to the snow's beauty. I'd certainly never witnessed its like in London's crowded, dirty streets.

But today I stared at the snow without really seeing it, too angry and scared by the morning's twists and turns to appreciate it. I'd reached a point so low that I almost wished to return to Miss Medleycoate's establishment. Perhaps the food was worse and the beds less warm and comfortable, but no ghosts roamed the orphanage's halls. I had Miss Beatty to comfort me and friends to laugh and talk with. I was often sad but never lonely or frightened. Here I was all three.

EIGHT

INALLY THE COLD DROVE ME to close the window and put on my own dress, rough and brown and scratchy against my skin. Afraid to stay in my room alone, I took my book and ran down to the sitting room and made myself comfortable in the big leather chair by the wood fire, much warmer than my coal fire.

I was so deeply immersed in *Vanity Fair* that I didn't notice Sophia until she exhaled her cold breath on my cheek. Startled, I dropped my book. "Go away," I begged. "I've had enough of you."

"But I haven't had enough of you, dear Florence." She perched on the arm of the chair and studied me with her dull eyes. "I see you've changed your clothes. Did you not like my dress?"

"I hate your dress!" I told her. "When James saw me wearing it, he thought I was you."

"Much more flattering to you than to me. Even dead, I'm far prettier than you are." She laughed her spooky little laugh and ran her bony fingers through her tufts of hair. Looking at me closely, she touched my nose. "Consider that bump in your nose: it's especially unattractive and bound to get worse as you age."

She jumped off the chair and did a few turns about the room, as graceful as a sylph in a ballet. Perhaps more so, for a living ballerina could not have floated as lightly as Sophia did.

"I must say, I enjoyed hearing Aunt's response to the sight of you in my dress," she said. "Poor old thing to mistake you for me—her eyesight must be failing."

She twirled around the room again, her ragged skirt floating around her. "I still have Aunt wrapped around my little finger, but she positively *detests* you."

"Why don't you haunt her and leave me alone?" I asked. "She'd be happy to see you."

"Aunt is a boring old bat. She was useful when I was alive, but now . . ." Sophia shrugged. "I have no need of pretty things or sweets. Indeed, it's a relief not to make a pretense of loving her. Why should I continue the charade by appearing to her?"

"You are the most wicked creature I've ever met," I whispered. Despite my own feelings toward Aunt, I was glad she hadn't known Sophia's true nature.

Sophia smiled as if I'd complimented her. Twirling back to the chair, she settled next to me, numbing me with cold. "Poor James is so afraid of me," she giggled. "Did he scream and cry and throw a tantrum at the sight of you?"

I tried to move away from her, but she kept me close to her. "He told me you want him to die," I said.

Sophia twirled a strand of hair around her finger and curled it into a ringlet. "I was cheated," she said. "James was meant to die, not me."

"How can you believe such a thing?" I asked. "No one knows who is meant to die and who is meant to live."

Clenching her fists in anger, Sophia jumped to her feet. "It's not fair! It's not fair! It's not fair!" she screamed like a small child. "Why should he be allowed to make me miserable even after I'm dead? Didn't he make me miserable enough while I was alive?"

Frightened by her anger, I cowered in the chair. "I cannot believe James ever caused you pain," I whispered.

"He was *born*, wasn't he? Isn't that enough?" Giving me a look of pure hatred, Sophia ran from the sitting room. Behind her, the fire died down, nearly extinguished by the draft of cold air she created.

As soon as she was gone, the flames on the hearth leapt up, snapping and crackling, but it took a long time for them to warm the icy air.

When I was certain I was alone, I drew my knees to my chest and curled up in the chair like a cat. I tried to lose myself in my novel, but instead of reading Thackeray's words, I heard Sophia's voice in my head, taunting me. What did she want with me? Could I really resist her? Or was James right about her being too strong for me to fight?

Just before the clock struck seven, Nellie appeared in the doorway. "Miss," she said almost fearfully, "I come to say dinner be ready and they be a-waiting on ye."

"Nellie." I ran to her side and took her arm. To

my dismay, she flinched as if she expected me to hit her. "Oh, Nellie, I am so sorry I spoke harshly to you. I don't know where those words came from. Please accept my apologies."

Nellie studied my face, her eyes troubled. "Ye scairt me, miss. I thought I'd done summat wrong to make ye so mad."

"No, you did nothing wrong." I gave her a quick hug. "I promise never to speak to you like that again."

Nellie nodded and darted out of the room as if I'd embarrassed her.

Behind me, I heard a mocking laugh. "You have the mind of a servant," Sophia whispered. "Soon you'll be helping that detestable girl with her chores."

A draft swept out of the room ahead of me and vanished into the shadows.

In the dining room, Uncle sat at the end of the table and Aunt sat at his right. They looked at me but neither smiled. Their faces were solemn. Indeed, Aunt's was grim.

"Sit down, Florence," Uncle said.

I sank into my chair across from Aunt. It was clear she'd told Uncle about my disobedience. Lowering my head, I toyed with my spoon, moving it to the right and back to the left. I had no appetite for the steaming soup in front of me.

"You know that James needs peace and quiet," Uncle said. "He must not be upset or disturbed in any way. Yet you entered his room without permission and frightened him."

"I'm very sorry, Uncle." My face burned with shame. Unable to meet his eyes, I kept my head down. "I never meant to harm James—I just wanted to meet him. I didn't think—"

"You are a thoughtless, selfish, disobedient girl," Aunt interrupted. "Excuses cannot change what you did. It is unforgivable."

"Now, Eugenie—" Uncle began.

"The girl is a troublemaker. I sensed it from the first." She took a deep breath and added, "If you need to be convinced, listen to what else Florence has done. She went to the attic and removed things from Sophia's trunk."

To my mortification, Aunt pulled Clara Annette from her lap and brandished the doll as if it were evidence in a criminal trial. "I found this hidden in a drawer in her bureau."

For a moment, we all stared at the doll as if we expected it to speak.

"The head is broken beyond repair," Aunt went on, nearly in tears. "It was Sophia's favorite, very expensive. I brought it home from Paris. A Madame Jumeau doll with a little trunk of clothing, made to order to match Sophia's wardrobe. And look at it. Look at it!" She shook the doll in Uncle's face.

Uncle tried to say something, but Aunt wasn't finished. "There's more. When I caught her in James's room, she was wearing Sophia's best dress. Then do you know what she did with it? Thrust it into the coal fire in her bedroom. She could have burned down the house!"

"That was very foolish." Uncle turned to me, clearly puzzled. "I don't understand your reason for burning the dress."

"I had to get rid of it," I wept. "I had to!"

"You see?" Aunt leaned toward her brother. "The girl doesn't have good sense. Who knows what she'll do next?"

Uncle shook his head sadly. "I do not understand," he repeated. "Your thoughtless act endangered us all."

"I recommend locking up the kitchen knives," Aunt said, her lips pursed so tightly, she could barely speak. "Next she might take it into her head to murder us in our beds."

"Now, now, Eugenie," Uncle said calmly, "you are on the verge of hysteria."

"I'm sorry." I wrung my hands in dread and remorse. "I'm truly, truly sorry, Uncle. If you wish to send me back to Miss Medleycoate, I'll go."

"Send you back to Miss Medleycoate?" Uncle stared at me. "Whatever gave you such an idea? You're my flesh and blood, Florence. I have no intention of sending you away."

"Except to boarding school," Aunt said primly. "We have agreed to that, brother. At Saint Ursula's Academy, Florence will be taught etiquette and deportment. She will cease reading novels and apply her mind to serious moral works."

Uncle Thomas winced at his sister's rising voice. "Perhaps we should discuss these issues at some other time," he said, "when we are all calmer. It's obvious that Florence is sorry she behaved thoughtlessly."

"*Thoughtlessly.*" Aunt looked heavenward as if seeking patience. "Her behavior is more than *thoughtless*, Thomas. In my opinion, it borders on malice."

Malice. I stared at my aunt. If she knew Sophia as well as she thought she did, she'd have a better idea of the difference between malice and thoughtlessness.

"She is clearly jealous of her cousin Sophia," Aunt went on. "Why else would she destroy her things and upset her brother? Poor, blameless Sophia, struck down in her youth and beauty by a cruel accident. How can anyone be jealous of a dead girl?"

"I am *not* jealous of Sophia," I said. "She—"

"Sophia was your superior in every way," Aunt interrupted, before I could tell her the truth about her precious Sophia. "Beauty, intelligence, grace, and rectitude," she went on. "Perfect manners, too."

Uncle frowned at his sister. "Sophia had her faults, Eugenie. We are all flawed. You as well as I."

"Speak for yourself, Thomas!"

Ignoring his sister, Uncle began to carve the roast. "Let us eat while the food is still hot." So saying, he passed a plate to me. "Please help yourself to potatoes and carrots, my dear."

Suddenly Aunt leaned across the table and tapped my hand sharply with a bony finger. "Have you begun reading *Pilgrim's Progress*?"

"No, I have not." I looked her in the eye as I spoke. "I do not care for it."

"You do not *care* for it." She shook her head. "I suppose you do not care for the state of your immortal soul either?"

"Eugenie, please." Uncle patted his sister's hand. "Allow the child to enjoy her dinner."

"As you wish, Thomas." Aunt rose from the table. "Please tell Nellie to bring my dinner to my room."

In the silence that followed her departure, the air settled around us comfortably.

"I'm sorry, Uncle," I said. "It seems I can do nothing to please Aunt."

"Don't blame yourself, Florence. Eugenie is not an easy person to please." He smiled at me. "Now stop fretting and eat your dinner. You don't want to disappoint Mrs. Dawson."

Pushing my cold soup aside, I picked at the food on my plate. What little I ate, I did not enjoy.

When Nellie came to clear the table, Uncle and I retreated to the sitting room and settled by the fire to read, he with a thick book of essays by Thomas Carlyle and I with *Vanity Fair*.

"Uncle," I said, "am I really to go to boarding school?"

He looked up from his book, his face rosy in the

firelight. "You need a proper education, Florence. You're obviously a highly intelligent girl."

"Couldn't you teach me here?"

"Me?" He chuckled. "I wouldn't have the slightest idea of where to begin. My mathematics are quite rusty, and my scientific knowledge is limited to the ancient Greeks."

"Aunt teaches James."

"Not very well, I fear." He looked at me closely. "I don't think you'd enjoy her methods."

"No, probably not." I snuggled deeper into my chair and watched the fire dance upon the logs, slowly consuming them.

"I've been considering hiring a governess for James," Uncle continued. "Eugenie is opposed to the idea, but she hasn't the skill to teach the boy more than the rudiments—which he has already mastered, as have you."

Remembering my cousin's hysterical behavior, I touched my uncle's hand. "Is James well enough to have a governess?"

"Yes, I think it will do him good." Uncle smiled at me. "She could give lessons to both of you. I can't think of anything better for him. Or for you."

Suddenly worried, I looked at Uncle anxiously. "Will James want to see me again?"

"I talked to him before dinner. He wants you to know he's sorry for his outburst."

"I'm relieved to hear that, Uncle. I would enjoy taking lessons with James." I paused a moment before asking an important question. "But will Aunt agree to my staying here? She seems determined to be rid of me."

Uncle contemplated the fire as if the words he needed might be found in its flames. "My sister often wants things she doesn't get," he said softly. "She hasn't had a happy life."

With an attempt at a cheerful smile, he turned to me. "I prefer to keep you here with James. So here you will stay. Tomorrow I shall begin my search for a suitable governess."

With that, he reopened his book and I reopened mine. For some time we read in silent harmony. It didn't matter that Sophia joined us. It didn't matter that she crept close and whispered, "Aunt might not get everything she wants, but I do." It didn't matter that she drew some of the warmth from the fire. With uncle beside me, I felt safe.

Going up to bed after supper was a different matter. Buried under a heap of quilts, I shivered as if I'd never be warm. Although I didn't see or hear her, I knew Sophia could be anywhere, visible or invisible, hiding in dark corners, watching and planning, mocking me, scaring me, a presence following me as closely as my own shadow.

NINE

N THE MORNING, I WENT down to breakfast feeling more tired than I'd been before I'd gone to bed. Sophia had chased me through dream after dream all night long. She wanted me to do something, she said I had to, and I knew I mustn't obey her. She was wicked, and the thing she wanted done was wicked too. I had to escape, but we were in the garden and she was here and there and everywhere. I couldn't get away from her. Or the thing she wanted me to do.

"You're up early," Mrs. Dawson said.

Yawning a great yawn, I reached for my teacup. "I had bad dreams."

"Never tell a dream before breakfast." Mrs. Dawson handed me a plate of bread, butter, and jam. "It's the surest way to make it come true."

I shuddered. "That's the last thing I want," I told Mrs. Dawson.

As I was finishing my oatmeal, I saw Nellie hesitating in the doorway as if she weren't sure of her welcome. I raised my hand and beckoned to her.

Like a mouse, she scurried across the room and slid into a place beside me. "I been thinking, miss," she whispered, eyeing Mrs. Dawson's broad back. Deciding the cook was intent on her chores, Nellie continued in a voice so low, I could barely hear her. "Maybe it were *her* that made ye speak so mean." As she spoke, her eyes darted around the room. "Her ain't here now, is her?"

I looked around uneasily. "No, not now."

"But her can come anytime her wants." Nellie laid a cold hand on mine. "I been feeling her meself. Like a shadow her be, dark and cold and hateful."

"Can you see her, Nellie?"

"Almost." Her body tense, Nellie peered about just as I had, checking dark doorways and corners. "Her scares me something terrible, miss."

"How long have you known about her, Nellie?"

"Her been comin' upon me slowly." Flustered, Nellie knocked a spoon off the table and onto the floor.

Surprised by the noise, Mrs. Dawson looked over her shoulder. "Are you finished with your chores, Nellie?"

"No'm. I come to fill me bucket." With that, Nellie scooted to the sink and pumped water into her scrub bucket. Giving me a small, scared smile, she hurried out of the kitchen.

Left on my own, I took my book to the sitting room and sat down to read. Before long, Sophia waltzed across the room, dipping and turning as if she actually had a partner.

"I don't believe you could dance a waltz," she said, "as untrained and clumsy as you are."

It was true. I'd never taken a dancing lesson. Miss Medleycoate had never encouraged any of us to imagine we might someday spin around a ball-room with a handsome suitor.

"I could play the piano with a precocity that amazed both Aunt and Uncle," Sophia went on. "I sang, too, but I am now sadly out of practice."

I looked at her with both pity and loathing. Pity because she was most certainly dead and not about to go dancing with anyone. Loathing because she was mean and spiteful and obviously had not benefitted morally from dying.

Pulling the drapes aside, Sophia peered at the snow. "Quick, put on your coat. I have a mind to build a snowman."

Although I was comfortable where I was, I found myself running to my room. When I returned with my coat, scarf, hat, and mittens, Sophia wrinkled her nose.

"If you were as I am now, you wouldn't need those cumbersome garments," she said. "You'd never be hot, never be cold, never be hungry or tired or afraid."

"I'd never be anything," I murmured.

Although I hadn't meant her to hear me, Sophia gave me a hateful look. "If justice prevails," she said, "I will soon be as you are." Under her breath, she added, "And James will be as I am."

"What do you mean?" I asked, but she merely laughed.

"Come along," she called. "I'm eager to build my snowman."

Nellie looked up as we ran through the scullery. She opened her mouth to speak but stopped, her face puzzled, then frightened. "Miss," she cried. "Miss!" But she didn't follow me.

Outside, Sophia darted across the snow and disappeared into the garden. She left no tracks, but I found her easily enough, waiting for me by the fountain. The stone children and their captive swan wore hats and coats of snow, and the words on the rim were hidden.

"This has always been my favorite place." Sophia brushed the snow off the fountain's rim and read the inscription. "Here and there and everywhere—it's a riddle," she said. "Do you know the answer?"

I shook my head, and she smiled. "Just as I thought. You're not nearly as clever as I am."

Leaning close to me, she chilled my cheek with her wintry breath. "Uncle says the answer is time, though he thinks it could also be the wind. But *I* know the true answer."

Sophia's eyes held mine. I couldn't turn away. "It's *Death*," she whispered. "Death is here and there and everywhere."

Sophia looked at the house, its dark stone almost black against the whiteness, its roof and tall chimneys blending into the sky. "You cannot escape death," she said softly. "You'll find out for yourself someday. Perhaps when you least expect it, he will come for you."

I drew away from her, burrowing my face into the warmth of my scarf. It was true. There was no escaping something you couldn't see, even if you knew where to look.

"I've scared you, haven't I?" Sophia's laugh was as brittle as the sound of ice breaking. "Start rolling a ball for the snowman. I want it to be as tall as the chimney tops."

She kept me working until my toes and fingers were numb from cold. Slowly the snowman took shape. Three balls of snow balanced one atop the other, not nearly as tall as the chimney tops, but lofty enough to see eye to eye with the stone children on their pedestal.

Sophia studied the snowman. "He needs a carrot for his nose and lumps of coal for his eyes and mouth. Run to the kitchen and come right back. Promise."

Obediently I darted through the snow and into the warmth of the kitchen. Stuffing a handful of coal into my pocket, I grabbed a carrot from the table.

"Here," Mrs. Dawson said. "Where are you

going with that carrot? I just pared it for to-night's stew."

"It's for the snowman we're building in the garden."

"'We'?" Mrs. Dawson looked at me in sur-prise. "You and who else? If Nellie is out there playing, you tell her to get herself inside. She has work to do."

A bit rattled by my slip, I shook my head. Mrs. Dawson would not want to hear about Sophia, wait-ing impatiently for me. "I'm building it. Just me. I don't know why I said 'we.'"

Mrs. Dawson held out an unpeeled carrot and I returned the one she'd pared. "Your lips are blue with cold, child. Stay inside a bit and warm up. The snowman can wait for his nose."

"No, I promised I'd be right back."

"Promised who?"

Without answering, I slipped out the door and ran to the garden. I didn't dare keep Sophia waiting.

"You took your time," Sophia said.

She watched me add the snowman's eyes, mouth, and nose. "No, no," she said crossly. "He mustn't smile."

Snatching the lumps of coal, Sophia rearranged them and stood back, with a grin. She'd transformed my creation. With frowning brows and a grim, down-turned mouth, he stared at me. He was fearsome, almost as frightening as Sophia herself.

"Perfect." She smiled and stepped back to admire her creature. "It will give everyone a start to see him standing here exactly where I built mine."

Suddenly she tensed as a cat does when it hears something no one else does. "Hide," she cried. "He's coming!"

Frightened, I followed Sophia into the yew trees around the fountain and huddled under the snowy branches. "Who's coming?" I whispered.

There was no answer. Sophia had vanished.

"Who be here?" Spratt called. "Come out and show yerself."

With some embarrassment, I crawled out from the yew tree. In doing so, I brushed against a branch that then dumped its load of snow on my head.

"Well, it be hard to say which be the girl and which be the snowman," Spratt said with a chuckle.

I brushed the snow off. My nose felt like the carrot in the snowman's face, frozen hard as diamonds.

While I stamped my feet to warm them, Spratt studied the snowman. "This be a right good job," he said, "but there's summat familiar about him." He put his hand on my shoulder. "Could it be ye had some help a-building it?"

When I didn't answer immediately, he went on, "I sees onliest one set of footprints. I reckon they be yers. *Her* don't leave no footprints."

"Sophia," I whispered. "*She* made his face."

"Hush, don't be saying her name. That's like inviting her to come." Spratt leaned on the shovel he'd been using to clear snow from the garden walk, and peered into my eyes. "Ye see her, do ye?"

I nodded. "First I felt her, then I heard her, and now I see her. She comes to my room, she follows me upstairs and down. No matter where I go, I can't escape her."

Spratt sighed and shook his head. "It be a shame for a child to be so wicked as that 'un. Wish I knowed a way to make her lie peaceful in her grave like most folk do."

"You gave James a charm to protect him. Can you make one for me?" My voice rose. "She wants him dead—she wants me dead too. She hates me. I tell you, she hates me!"

"No, no. Her just be toying with ye. It's always been her way to taunt and tease and hurt." He paused and stared at the snowman, its tall shape white against the darkening sky. "It be Master James her wants to harm, not ye. But we won't let her get to him, will we? We'll keep a close watch, ye and me."

My teeth chattered so hard that I couldn't speak. Sophia was the cat and James and I were the mice. When she was tired of playing with us, she'd bite off our heads and eat us.

"Poor lass, ye be just about froze." Spratt took my hand. "Let me take ye back to the house. Be dark soon. Mr. Crutchfield will be a-looking for ye."

In the dusky light of a winter afternoon, the land rolled away toward the distant hills, its whiteness shading into a bluish gray. The snow creaked under our feet, but ahead, the hall's windows glowed with warmth. Hot tea would be waiting by the fire in the sitting room, along with bread and butter and jam.

Behind us, Sophia hid in the snow-laden garden, watching me, smiling that spiteful smile. She would come inside when she wished, but she'd drink no tea, she'd eat no bread and jam. All the fires in the house could not warm her bones. Alone, she'd twirl through the house like a cold draft, thinking of nothing but ways to make James pay for her death.

TEN

LL NIGHT LONG, THE WIND
blew and Sophia pursued me into my
dreams as she had the night before.
Awake or asleep, I could not escape her.

Exhausted, I dragged myself down to breakfast
and sank into my seat at the kitchen table.

Mrs. Dawson looked at me sharply. "Bad
dreams again?"

I nodded and she clucked her tongue. "Poor child.
You'll be needing a good dose of my special tonic."

Nellie slid in beside me. "Don't take none of
that," she said. "It be poison for certain."

"Hmm," Mrs. Dawson said. "Looks like you
could use some yourself, Nellie dear."

"It's me dreams," Nellie said. "Lately they be a-wearing me out."

She looked out the window at the snow-blanketed garden. "It were on account of that snowman you made, miss. I seen it afore I went to bed, a-standing in the garden, looking like the devil hisself. Why'd ye make him so big and scarifying?"

Mrs. Dawson joined Nellie at the window. "It's strange, but Sophia built a snowman just like that on the day before she died. She told James the snowman would come to life at night and steal him from his bed. He'd bury James deep in the snow. No one would ever see him again. She terrified the poor—"

"Stop, mistress, stop!" Nellie cowered at the table, her hands pressed to her ears. "That be just what I dreamed, only it were me the snowman took."

Wide awake now, I stared at Nellie and then turned to Mrs. Dawson. "I dreamed the same thing," I whispered. "The snowman dragged me to the churchyard and laid me in a grave and heaped snow over me."

By now, Nellie had her apron over her head and was sobbing. "Yes, yes, he took me to the churchyard too, and he buried me under the snow, and I couldn't dig me way out or move or cry for help. I wanted to come home so bad."

Mrs. Dawson's face lost its ruddy color. "The day Sophia was buried it snowed again. They'd no sooner shoveled the dirt onto her grave than the snow covered her. I couldn't help thinking how cold she must be." Her hands shook, and tea slopped over the rim of her cup.

She moved closer to the fire. "Poor child." Mrs. Dawson crossed herself. "Poor, cold child." She glanced at a calendar hanging on the wall and crossed herself again. "It was on this very day she died. Twelve months ago, a whole year now."

As she spoke, I felt Sophia creep up behind me. Her cold breath lifted the hair on my neck. No one saw her, not even me, but she was there in the kitchen, making the fire on the hearth flicker and flare.

Mrs. Dawson shivered. "There's a draft in here today, worse than usual. Makes my old bones ache."

"Sophia were a wicked 'un," Nellie whispered.

The air quivered, and a heavy stoneware pitcher fell from a shelf. Just missing Nellie's head, it shattered harmlessly on the stone floor.

"See what happens when you speak ill of the dead?" Mrs. Dawson bent to clean up the shards of china. "Show me a perfect child, Nellie, before you criticize Sophia."

For a moment, Nellie sat still and stared at Mrs. Dawson and the broken pitcher. Then she and I looked at each other. We both knew the pitcher had not fallen by accident.

Mrs. Dawson dumped the remains of the pitcher into the trash bin. "You have work to do, Nellie. Master wants his boots polished, and the floors need sweeping and the fires must be tended."

Nellie ran off, glad to leave the kitchen where Sophia lingered unseen. "If I was you," Mrs. Dawson said to me, "I'd busy myself with needlework or knitting, maybe even read the Bible and say some prayers. Remember, Satan casts his nets far and wide. And you aren't as smart as you think you are."

Behind me, Sophia chilled my neck with her breath again. Mrs. Dawson drew her shawl more tightly around her shoulders and rose to put more wood on the fire. "I've never known this kitchen to be so cold."

I excused myself to fetch a wrap, but as soon as I left the kitchen, Sophia stepped in front of me. "I have a mind to show you something."

Even though I struggled to resist her, Sophia

seized my hand and dragged me outside. Snow had begun to fall again, and a strong wind made a din in the treetops. I tried to hang back, but my cousin dragged me away from the house. "Where are we going?" I cried. "I need my coat, my hat."

Sophia did not answer. Clad only in her thin silk dress, she struck out across the snow, pulling me with her. From time to time, the wind lifted her off her feet and threatened to carry her away, but it never succeeded. Somehow she stayed on, or close to, the ground. Perhaps my weight held her down— I did not know, could not tell.

Faster she ran and faster still, dragging me behind her. The wind bit my face, and sprays of flying snow blinded me. "Please," I cried, "go slower. I cannot keep up with you."

With a laugh, Sophia glanced over her shoulder, her face stark white. "The living are not as light on their feet as the dead."

On we went, across fields, up hills and down, skirting a pond, ducking under tree limbs heavy with snow. Using the last of my strength, I followed Sophia to a hilltop where the wind blew so savagely, I thought it might carry us across the sea to America. Just below us lay a small huddle of houses, a couple of shops, an inn, and a church. The scene reminded me of a Christmas village I'd seen once in a shop window.

"Lower Bolton," Sophia said.

I said nothing, but I was cheered by the thought that living people were nearby. Fires and hot tea and warm food. Comfort. If only I could escape Sophia and seek a kindly person to help me.

Tightening her grip on my wrist, Sophia glided downhill toward the village, slowed only by my stumbling gait. When we reached the churchyard, I was prepared to collapse and freeze to death in a snowbank.

Sophia smirked. "That's the price you pay for dragging your cumbersome body everywhere you go."

Too weary to speak, I followed her through the gate. We wound our way through a city of tombstones, some taller than I was, some in danger of falling, some already fallen. The inscriptions on many were too weathered to read, and the stones were black against the white snow. It was a desolate place on a winter day.

Sophia stopped beside a stone about her height, capped with snow. With a dramatic gesture, she pointed to the inscription, its letters crisply cut and recently done:

Here Lies
Sophia Mary Crutchfield
Only Daughter of William and Susannah
15 September 1871 to 27 January 1883
Our Loss, Heaven's Gain

"Aunt's doing," Sophia said. "She's one of the few who believed I'd go to Heaven. Poor old thing—she was so easily duped."

"Someone left flowers." I pointed to a half-dozen roses as red as blood against the white snow.

"Aunt again." Sophia picked up a rose and watched it turn black in her fingers. "As Dawson remarked, today's my death-day. Twenty-seven January. Exactly one year ago."

She glanced at me slyly. "Odd, isn't it? You know when your birthday is, but not your death-day, even though you pass the date year after year, never suspecting that someday . . ." She smiled and left the thought unfinished.

I'd pondered the same thing myself many times.

Indeed, I supposed most people wondered what date would mark their life's end.

"I don't suppose you like to think of the period at the end of the sentence," Sophia said.

I shrugged and pulled the collar of my dress tightly around my neck. No matter what I did, I could not keep out the wind. Its busy fingers squeezed between my buttons and pushed their way up my sleeves and funneled down my neck.

"Should we celebrate my death-day? With gifts and cake and song?"

I shook my head and said nothing. I wanted my coat, my scarf, my hat. I wanted to be home, safe and warm by the fire, reading my book.

"No, I suppose one does not celebrate one's death-day." For a moment Sophia seemed to sink into sorrow, but then she brightened. "Here's something I'm certain you do not know. The dead are strongest on their death-days, just as the living are weakest on their birthdays."

"Nonsense. I'm no weaker on my birthday than any other day."

Sophia looked at me sharply. "Don't you feel strangely vulnerable on your birthday? As if the force that birthed you can take you back on the same day?"

"Sometimes," I admitted, "but I don't understand why it should be so."

"There's much you don't understand," Sophia said. "This part I will tell you. I've watched and I've waited for this day, feeling myself strengthen as the months passed. At first I could not crawl out of my coffin, just as a baby cannot crawl out of its cot. It took me a month to climb from my grave, but at first I could do no more than creep around the graveyard like a loathsome worm. By June, I was standing and soon walking. In July, exactly six months after my death-day, I made my way home and began to terrify James. Spratt set me back when he made that charm, but at least I'd made certain James was not enjoying the life he stole from me."

She paused and smiled, revealing the rotten little stumps of her teeth. "Then you arrived, dear cousin," she said, "and I knew if I waited until my death-day I'd be strong enough to make you do whatever I wished."

"No." I shook my head. "No, no." But I heard the weakness in my voice, and so did Sophia.

Turning back to her grave, Sophia said, "Just

imagine, if you will, that the inscription reads 'Here Lies James Ernest Crutchfield, Only Son of William and Susannah, 20 July 1873 to 27 January 1883—Our Loss, Heaven's Gain.'"

She paused a moment to allow me time to imagine. "And then," she said, "imagine I stand here beside you, a living girl, telling you the sad story of my brother's untimely death."

I wrapped my arms tightly across my chest, unwilling to picture James dead and Sophia alive. "That's not the way it happened," I whispered.

She glared at me. "I tell you, it is the way it *should* have happened!"

"No—"

"Yes!" She held my wrist so tightly, I felt the sharpness of her bones dig into my flesh. "Think of your body buried deep in the earth, lying there in the cold and the dark, day in and day out, for a whole year. Spring, summer, fall, and winter again. Stars wheeling overhead, the moon and the sun rising and setting, grass growing and dying, and the snow returning. Would you not want to be free of the grave? To live again? No matter who paid the cost?"

I gazed at the grave, knowing I would not want to lie where Sophia's body lay, knowing I wanted to live as long as I could. Pitying her, pitying me, pitying all of us, I hugged my living self as tightly as I could.

Sophia stared at me from her dull dark eyes. "How can you blame me for wanting what everyone wants?"

I shook my head, unable to answer.

"Why should James live and I die? Is he better than I am? Is he more valuable than I am?" Sophia grabbed my arms and forced me to look at her. "I tell you, he does not deserve to live! He took everything from me—he owes me his life."

Fed by her own fury, Sophia began to run once more, towing me behind her again. Headstones spun away from us, the churchyard gate flew open, homes and shops blurred as we ran past them, away from the church, away from the village, up the road toward Crutchfield Hall.

ELEVEN

HE SNOWY GROUND SLID AWAY beneath my feet as if I were ice skating, faster and faster until I was sure we'd left the ground altogether and were flying on the wind. When I inhaled, the cold air burned my lungs and drew tears from my eyes. My forehead ached as if it were packed in ice.

At last Crutchfield Hall came into view, its dark stone walls a welcome sight. Down one last hill, across the lawn and the terrace, and through the door we went, Sophia leading, me following.

When Sophia released her grip on me, my legs were as weak as a baby's and my knees shook. I slid to the floor and leaned against the wall, certain I'd never stand or walk again.

"I thought you'd enjoy a fast trip home," Sophia said, "but I see your body is simply not up to it."

"Please, I want to go to my room now," I whispered. "I need to lie down and rest and recover my senses."

"Not yet." Seizing my hand again, Sophia pulled me to my feet and led me upstairs and down the hall to James's room.

"Why are we stopping here?" I asked.

"So you may enter the room and remove the charm over the door, the one Samuel Spratt put there. Be very quiet. My brother must not see you."

"No, I won't do it." My voice shook and my limbs trembled. I had to force myself to defy her. "The charm is there to protect James from you."

"You must not oppose me on my death-day." With a smirk, Sophia added, "I wish to see my brother—whether he wants to see me or not."

Although I did not intend to obey her, I found myself turning the knob slowly and quietly. I knew I shouldn't open the door, I knew I was endangering

James, I knew I couldn't trust Sophia, but I could not resist her. It was her death-day. She stood behind me, a force I lacked the strength to resist.

The room was dim. James was curled on his side, his back to the door, apparently sleeping. I turned my eyes from him. I couldn't bear to see him lying there, trusting in a charm to keep him safe.

Slowly I reached above the door and fumbled in the dust and cobwebs for the charm. It was no more than a bundle of twigs, moss, and dried flowers tied together with a green ribbon, so little a thing to keep Sophia away. Holding it tightly, I stepped back into the hall and closed the door behind me.

When Sophia saw what I had, she took a step backwards. "Get rid of it," she hissed. "It reeks of comfrey and hyssop and other vile things."

"What should I do with it?"

"Throw it out the window at the end of the corridor," Sophia ordered. "Be quick!"

With an aching heart, I went to the window, opened the casement, and flung the little bundle as far as I could. I watched it fall into the snow and vanish. "Wrong," I whispered. What I'd just done was wrong. Why hadn't I stopped myself?

Turning back, I saw Sophia slip into James's room. Filled with dread, I hurried after her.

She stood beside the bed looking down at the sleeping boy. "He's grown taller," she whispered, "but he's frail and thin and almost as insubstantial as I am." Her voice was scornful.

"He's ill," I reminded her.

Sophia studied her brother's face. "First he killed our mother and shortly thereafter our father. Then he killed me. I tell you, he deserves to die."

"Your mother died in childbirth, and your father died of fever," I reminded her. "James isn't responsible for either. If he had anything to do with *your* death, it was accidental."

James stirred and slowly opened his eyes. He saw me first. "Florence," he murmured, "I was sleeping."

"Have you nothing to say to me?" Sophia leaned over her brother, her face inches from his.

"Sophia!" James looked at her with horror. "You cannot come here. The charm—"

Sophia smiled. "Our sweet cousin did my bidding and removed Spratt's silly old contrivance."

James stared at me. "How could you have done so?"

I shook my head, too ashamed to answer or even to look at him.

"I *made* her do it," Sophia said. "Everyone does what I say. You know that."

"I'm sorry," I whispered to James. "Truly, I am."

"Enough jibber-jabber," Sophia said. "Do you know what today is, James?"

"Today?" He thought a moment, his forehead as creased as an old man's. "It's January twenty-seventh," he said in a low voice.

"Does that date have any significance for you?"

He plucked the edge of his blanket with nervous fingers. "It's the day you died," he whispered.

Sophia made him repeat himself three times until she was satisfied he'd spoken loudly enough. "Now answer this. Who is stronger today, you or I?"

James slid deeper into his bed until he was almost totally covered by blankets. "You are" came the muffled reply.

Sophia pulled back the covers, revealing her brother's shaking body. "I didn't hear you," she said. "Answer me again. Who is stronger today—you or I?"

"You are," James sobbed. "You are."

I touched her arm. "Please, Sophia," I begged. "Don't torment him. You'll make him sicker."

She shrugged me off. "I do not care how sick he is. He has not long to live." Turning to James, she said, "Get out of bed and dress yourself."

"I can't," he whimpered.

"Do as I say. Now!"

"No, Sophia." I tried to thrust myself between them, but she shoved me aside as if I were made of paper.

Dragging James from his bed, she said, "We're going somewhere, you and I. We have things to settle."

Shoving me out of her way, she opened the door and looked up and down the corridor. Seeing no one, she took James's hand and ran with him the way she'd run with me, fairly flying down the hall and up the stairs to the third floor.

TWELVE

FOLLOWED THEM AS FAST AS I could, but when I reached the top step, they had vanished. Breathing hard, I listened to my heart pound.

"Sophia," I called. "James. Where are you?"

As I waited for an answer, I heard creaking sounds over my head. Footsteps, I thought. In the attic.

I ran to the door and climbed the stairs so quickly, I tripped on the top step. Sprawled on the attic floor, I saw one pair of footprints in the dust, small and shoeless. I scrambled to my feet and followed them to an open window. When I poked my head out, I saw my cousins on the roof.

Frightened nearly to death, I climbed through the window and crept upward, slowly and cautiously. The wind had blown the snow off the slates, a good thing, but it tugged at my clothing and my hair. Worse yet, it billowed under my dress, threatening to lift me into the air like a balloon.

"Well, well." Sophia eyed me from her perch on the roof's highest point. "Here comes Cousin Florence. I thought you'd be afraid to follow us."

James huddled a few inches away from his sister, weeping. "Go back, Florence," he sobbed. "Go back."

"Oh, stay, cousin, stay," Sophia said. "And bear witness to an amazing feat. They say the past cannot be changed, what's done is done, but I mean to prove them wrong. Yes, that's what I mean to do."

Steadying myself against the side of a tall chimney, I stared at Sophia. "I don't understand," I said.

"Let me tell you our history at Crutchfield Hall," my cousin said. "We came here when I was ten and James was eight. Aunt was fond of me, but Uncle preferred James. He doted on him and took his side when we quarreled. Whatever James wanted, he was given—a book, a top, a ball, a dog, anything at all."

Sophia shot a venomous look at her brother,

whose face was as white as the fields stretching out to the horizon.

"You killed my dog," he whispered.

"Tut. I threw a ball. Is it my fault the dog was stupid enough to run in front of that cart?"

"You did it on purpose. You saw the cart and you threw the ball."

"You're a stupid little boy. Ask Aunt. She'll tell you it was an accident."

"Aunt wasn't there. It was just you and I." James's voice was getting stronger. Despite the wind and the flying snow, he faced his sister. "Spratt knew the truth. So did Uncle, even if he wouldn't dare say it."

"James, James, James," Sophia chanted, giving his name a nasty sound in the cold air. "*Everyone* adored James. Spratt, Uncle, the servants, the vicar, the village shopkeepers, the blacksmith. When James and I were together, no one noticed me. I was invisible."

"If you'd smiled more," James said tentatively, "if you hadn't been so sullen, then maybe people would have—"

"What did *I* have to smile about?" Sophia turned on James angrily. "My dear darling mother died giving birth to *you!* A brother I neither asked for nor wanted. And what a fuss they all made about the poor, motherless babe, without a thought for me, the poor, motherless girl. Father forgot about me—he paid me no mind at all. He cared only for you. Believe me: I had nothing to smile about and great reason to be sullen."

James had nothing more to say. Frightened, he stared at his sister. His lips shaped the word "please." But he did not say it. We both knew "please" meant nothing to Sophia.

Against my will, I looked down at the ground. Covered in new-fallen snow, the terrace lay far below. Spratt and his helper, a boy about my age, were no bigger than dolls as they went about their business. Dizzy with vertigo, I turned back to Sophia.

"Why have you chosen the roof to settle your quarrel?" I asked her.

She looked at James with contempt. "On this very day, I dared the little ninny to walk the ridge of the roof at its highest point, from this chimney to that one."

She pointed to a chimney about fifteen feet from the one James clung to. "He said he'd do it if I did it first." With a fierce scowl, she turned to her brother. "Didn't you say that? Didn't you?"

James nodded. He'd begun to cry again. His nose ran.

"You *promised.*"

"Yes," he whispered, "yes, I did. I promised to do it if you did it first."

"So I did—just like this." Sophia walked along the roof to the other chimney, touched it, and came back. The wind made her waver as if she were a paper doll, but she didn't fall. "You see? I did it then and I can do it now."

I supposed if one didn't look down, it wouldn't be too difficult to walk along the roof line. But how could one not think about the height of the roof and the certainty of death if one fell? I could never do such a foolish thing, no matter who dared me.

Sophia sneered at James. "Now it's your turn. Let's see if you can keep your promise this time."

"No," James sobbed. "I couldn't do it then and I cannot do it now. Please, Sophia, please, I'm sorry. It's my fault, all my fault. Blame it on me. Say I killed you. Say I deserve to suffer, but don't make me walk to the chimney. I cannot do it!"

Sophia was implacable. "I'm giving you a second chance, James. Not everyone is that fortunate."

"No, no—I cannot!"

Sophia tried to force him to stand. "Hold my hand. We'll do it together."

But James resisted. "I won't. You can't make me."

"You must do what you promised." She tugged at his hands as if to break his grip on the chimney.

"Please, stop," I begged. "Do you want to kill him?"

Sophia turned to me. Never had I seen a more malevolent expression on anyone's face. "Haven't I told you that already? Did you not believe me? Of course I want him to die," she said, "as he should have last year. I was stronger than he was—I was more agile. I had the grace and daring he lacked. What happened was a twist of fate, and I plan to correct it."

"You cannot correct anything," I said.

"You're wrong, cousin." Sophia gave me a scornful smile. "If James falls from the roof and dies today, I shall live. I know I shall. I must!"

I looked up at her wavering on the roof line, a small figure against a turbulent winter sky.

"If James falls, he will be dead," I cried, "and so will you. You can go on fighting for all eternity, but neither of you will ever return to life."

"You'll see." Sophia managed to pull James to his feet.

I watched my cousins struggle. The wind tugged at them almost as if it wanted them both to fall. James teetered, Sophia swayed. He leaned one way, she the other.

"Stop," I cried. "Stop!"

But they paid me no heed. Indeed, I don't think they heard me. Or remembered I was there.

Suddenly James pulled free of Sophia's grasp and tried to retreat. Hands outstretched, she came after him. Terrified, he pushed her away.

Sophia stumbled, her feet slipped on the slates, and she slid down the roof. With a scream, she shot off the edge and disappeared.

"It's just like before," James cried. "I pushed her and she fell. I killed her—I killed my sister!" Sobbing, he pressed his face against the chimney.

Cautiously, I peered over the edge of the roof. Sophia did not lie on the terrace below. She was gone.

With my heart pounding, I inched my way up the slates, struggling to find finger and toe holds. My fingers were so numb with cold, I expected to fall as Sophia had, but somehow I managed to join James by the chimney.

Putting my arms around him, I said, "You didn't mean for Sophia to fall. You were protecting yourself. It was an accident."

With a sob, James pulled away from me. "I must do as I promised. Perhaps I should have died and Sophia should have lived. I have to find out."

Ignoring my cries of protest, he began walking toward the other chimney. Step by step, slowly putting one foot just in front of the other, arms spread for balance, he teetered and tottered along the roof's ridge. The wind tugged at his nightgown, and his hair streamed behind him.

"No, James," I shouted. "Come back! You'll fall!"

He didn't answer; nor did he obey. He kept going with agonizing slowness, swaying as if he might lose his balance at any moment. Somehow he stayed upright. Unable to watch any longer, I covered my eyes and braced myself for his scream.

"Open your eyes and look," James cried. "Look at me!"

With great relief, I saw him touch the other chimney. Now all he had to do was return to me safely. Holding my breath, I watched him begin to make his slow and careful way back. Despite the wind, he kept his footing. Above him, clouds heavy with snow rolled across the sky. Below, crows as black as coal cawed in the trees.

At last, James's fingers touched the chimney. "I did it," he whispered. "I kept my promise, and I didn't fall." Exhausted, he sank down beside me.

"You were very brave." I hugged him, loving the warmth and solid feel of him, the life in his small body. *My brother*, I thought. *He's my brother now. I'll take better care of him than his real sister did.*

"But you were very foolish, too," I added in a whisper.

"Don't you see?" he asked. "I had to prove *I* wasn't meant to die. It was the only way to free myself from her."

I shivered in a blast of cold wind. "Do you think she's gone now?"

James looked at me, a long look that required no words. We both knew we weren't done with Sophia and she wasn't done with us. Her fall hadn't killed her. No one can die twice. She would return.

THIRTEEN

T THAT MOMENT, SPRATT looked up and saw us. "Stay where ye be," he yelled. "Don't take one step. I be sending the boy with a ladder."

While James and I huddled together, Spratt and his helper ran up to the attic. They managed to lay a ladder across the slates from the window to the roof's ridge. The boy climbed out on the slates and crawled up the ladder until he reached our perch. First he helped James climb down the ladder to the attic window. Once my cousin was safely inside, the boy returned for me. Spratt held my hands and guided me inside.

Uncle and Aunt were waiting in the attic. At the

sight of us, Uncle ran to embrace both James and me, but Aunt stood aside, her face tight with anger.

Pulling me away from Uncle, she shook me. "How could you do such a thing? And on this day, the very day Sophia died!"

"It's not Florence's fault," James cried. "It was Sophia. She made us do it."

Hearing this, both Aunt and Uncle forgot me and turned to James in consternation. "James, James," Uncle cried. "Your sister cannot make you do anything now. She's dead and gone. Please don't say such things."

"The boy is in a state of shock, and no one to blame but her." Aunt pointed at me. "I don't know what she's up to, but I tell you she's the devil's own."

Uncle ignored his sister. "You," he said to Spratt, "hurry to the village and fetch Dr. Fielding. I fear my nephew will have a seizure."

Spratt scowled at Aunt. "The boy be telling the truth. It were her, all right."

"You daft old man," Aunt cried. "Be quiet and fetch the doctor."

Spratt stood his ground, his brows lowered, his face flushed. "I tell ye, that girl be here yet, a-lurkin' and a-sneakin' and tryin' to do mischief to the little lad. Jealousy be stronger than death, as any fool knows."

"I'll not listen to this." Aunt turned away, her hands clasped. "It's a torment to be reminded of my darling's death."

Uncle took Spratt's arm. "Samuel," he said. "Get the doctor!"

"Yes, sir." Spratt hurried past Aunt and ran down the attic steps. Carrying James, Uncle followed close at his heels.

"Florence," he called, "find Nellie and tell her to build up a good fire for Master James. He'll need hot tea, too."

Eager to escape Aunt's baleful eye, I ran to fetch Nellie and Mrs. Dawson.

Halfway down the steps, Sophia stopped me with a cold hand on my shoulder.

"Now do you see how I suffered?" she whispered. "Nobody showed concern for me, just as nobody shows concern for *you*. Did anyone ask if you were cold or hurt? Oh, no. It was go fetch tea for *James*, Florence. Make sure the fire is warm enough for *James*, Florence. *James*, *James*, *James*. Always and forever, *James*, *James*, *James*."

I wheeled and faced Sophia. "Of course Uncle is worried about James. He's been in bed so long, it's a wonder he has any strength. He needs a doctor. I don't. Why shouldn't he come first?"

Sophia stared at me, her features twisted with anger. "You're on my brother's side, too. When will anyone ever be on my side?"

"Aunt is on your side."

"But I do not care for Aunt. She's such a tiresome old thing. Manners, deportment, etiquette, never a smile or a laugh or even a hug. How dreary it was to sit and play the piano for her. So much effort on my part simply to win a doll or a dress or a pair of fancy slippers. It wasn't what I wanted!"

Sophia withdrew further into the shadows, weeping now. It seemed to me she was dissolving like a paper doll in the rain, blurring, wavering. I could barely see her. But I could hear her.

"I wanted someone to love me the way they loved James," she sobbed. "That's all! If he hadn't been here, maybe someone would have loved me. But no, he took everyone's love and left me nothing. Nothing, nothing at all!"

With a wail of sorrow, Sophia vanished and I was

alone on the stairs. All that was left of her was an aching emptiness, a loneliness that hung in the air where she had disappeared.

"The tea," Aunt called to me from the top of the stairs. "You were to tell Nellie to bring tea and stoke the fire! Why are you still lingering on the stairs? Have you no sense? Do you not care what happens to James?"

Without answering, I ran to the kitchen and found Nellie scrubbing the kitchen floor. "Quick," I said. "Fix a good, hot fire in James's room, and bring hot tea for him."

Nellie wiped her small red hands on her apron. "What's happened, miss?"

"Never you mind," Mrs. Dawson said. "Fetch the coal."

"Yes'm." Nellie ran to the scullery.

Mrs. Dawson looked at me. "I knew there'd be trouble today. It was her, wasn't it? Causing mischief like she used to."

Before I could answer, she said, "No, don't tell me. I don't want to know." Grabbing a tray, she added, "Run along. I'll bring the tea."

I left Mrs. Dawson in the kitchen and slowly climbed the stairs. Poor Sophia. Poor pitiful, sad

Sophia. Had she gone uncomforted to her grave? I thought of her tombstone, already tilting over her grave, her name, her birth and death dates. What a short life. What an unhappy life.

Anxious to escape my thoughts, I went to James's room. Uncle had gotten him into bed and heaped blankets over him. "More coal on the fire," he barked at Nellie. "Build it up and drive away the chill."

As I approached the bed, Aunt took my arm. "What are you doing here? Your presence is not required."

As she began to usher me to the door, James stopped her with a cry. "Please let Florence stay," he begged. "Please."

"Hasn't she caused enough mischief already?" Aunt asked.

Pushing Uncle's hands away, James sat up in bed. "I tell you, this is Sophia's fault. *She* made Florence and me go to the roof. *She* wanted—"

"Nonsense!" Aunt exclaimed. "Sophia rests in peace as do all the dead. No one returns from the grave. It is heresy to think so."

Uncle gazed at his sister, his face solemn. "You heard what Samuel Spratt said, Eugenie. Perhaps there is some truth in this talk."

"Are you mad, brother?" Aunt tightened her grip on my arm. "The boy is ill, the girl is a liar, and Samuel Spratt is a superstitious, ignorant old man."

"Please, Aunt," I said. "You're hurting me."

"Release Florence," Uncle said. "James wishes her to stay."

"Then *I* shall depart!" With that, Aunt left the room in such haste that she almost bumped into Mrs. Dawson, who had chosen that moment to appear with the tea tray.

Mrs. Dawson set the tray down and beckoned to Nellie. "Come—you left the kitchen floor half scrubbed."

Touching Uncle's hand as she passed, Nellie whispered, "I ain't seen her, master, but she be here a-watching us all."

Uncle nodded. "Yes, my dear," he said softly. "I'm beginning to believe my niece haunts this house. There have been times when I . . ." His voice trailed off and he gazed into the fire. "Even Mr. Dickens believed in ghosts, I daresay. And Shakespeare, too. Who is to say what is real and what is not?"

Nellie glanced about fearfully. "Don't be saying too much about spirits, sir. Some folks say talking of the dead brings them out of their graves and into a house. They wants a warm place, too, I expect. The burial ground be powerful cold."

"That's quite enough, Nellie." Mrs. Dawson took the girl's arm and led her toward the door. "Beg your pardon, sir. We're all a bit unsettled."

"It's perfectly all right, Dawson." His face thoughtful, Uncle leaned back in his chair and watched Nellie follow Mrs. Dawson out of the room.

For a while we all sat in silence, drinking our tea and staring into the fire.

At last Uncle spoke. "Did not Mr. Shakespeare say 'There are more things in heaven and earth than are dreamt of in your philosophy, Horatio'—or something to that effect?"

"In *Hamlet*," I said. "After the ghost of Hamlet's father came to say he was murdered."

Uncle looked at me, pleased. "You've read Shakespeare, have you?"

"A few plays," I said. "I didn't completely understand them, so I plan to read them again when I'm older and know more about life."

Uncle chuckled. "What fun a governess will have with you and James."

James frowned as if he did not like the change of subject. "What we told you is true, Uncle. Sophia forced me to go to the roof."

"She thought she could change the past," I said. "She wanted James to fall and die so she could live."

"But it happened exactly the same way it did before," James said. "Sophia fell and I didn't."

"She's jealous of James," I said, "and she always has been. She thinks no one loved her." I paused and stared into the darkness beyond the firelight, wondering if Sophia was there now, listening. Overcome with pity, I dropped my voice to a whisper. "Sophia's very lonely. And very sad."

Uncle sighed. "I hope our loneliness and sorrow does not follow us to the grave and torment us there as it did in life. I've always thought of death as a release from mortal cares, but if what you say is true, my dear Florence, my philosophy, like Horatio's, must be reexamined."

Our conversation was interrupted by a knock on the door, followed by the entrance of Dr. Fielding. His face was ruddy from the cold, and the fresh smell of a winter evening clung to him.

"Well, well, young man," he said to James. "I understand you've been so foolish as to venture onto the roof again."

"It wasn't my idea," James began, but stopped when Uncle shook his head and frowned at him.

"Not your idea?" Dr. Fielding looked at him inquisitively.

James interested himself in the loose thread in his blanket, plucking at it to avoid looking at the doctor.

"It was my idea," I said quickly. "I wanted to see the place where Sophia fell, but I didn't expect James to climb up on the roof. I thought he would point from the window."

Dr. Fielding looked at me as if he'd noticed me for the first time. "So you followed him in case he needed rescuing?"

"Yes, sir." My cheeks burned with shame at telling a lie.

Turning to Uncle, Dr. Fielding said, "The girl bears an amazing resemblance to Sophia."

"Physically, yes," Uncle said. "But she is of an entirely different temperament."

A look passed between the two men, and Dr. Fielding took a seat on the edge of the bed. Taking

James's wrist, he felt his pulse. "Quite normal," he said. "How do you feel?"

"I feel surprisingly well, sir, though a bit tired from so much exertion."

Dr. Fielding listened to James's chest with his stethoscope, examined his throat, and finally leaned back with a smile and pronounced him much improved.

"Although I do not recommend doing it again, I must say, climbing the roof seems to have been good for you."

"I have no intention of doing it again, sir," said James.

"I am very glad to hear it," Uncle said.

Dr. Fielding nodded in agreement. "I suggest a day of rest tomorrow. Your aunt and uncle should watch for signs of a chill or some other adverse reaction to today's activities."

"Would it be possible for me to rest downstairs in the sitting room?" James asked. "I've grown weary of my bedroom."

"That's a splendid suggestion," said Uncle. "Do you give your permission, Fielding?"

"Wholeheartedly. James has spent entirely too much time in bed. Hopefully he'll soon be outside playing in the garden with Florence." Dr. Fielding patted James on the head. "But stay warm."

Uncle kissed James and left the room with Dr. Fielding. Alone, James and I sat on the bed and gazed at the fire. Outside, the wind blew harder. The snow seemed to have turned to ice from the noise it made striking the windows.

James yawned and snuggled under his covers. "I'm so tired," he whispered.

Curling up beside him, I peered into the corners where the shadows were darkest. Nothing stirred there. Nothing spoke. The fire murmured, and the sleet rattled the windowpanes. For a moment, I imagined I saw Sophia making her way through the night, her thin form battered by the wind. Slowly she walked, her head down. She paused at the churchyard gate, rimmed in ice now, and looked back as if she could see me from where she stood. Never had I witnessed such unhappiness, such loneliness, such despair.

Gradually Sophia faded out of sight among the crooked rows of tombstones. Moving close to James, I put one arm around him and fell into a deep sleep.

FOURTEEN

WAKENED BY A RAPPING ON
the door, I sat up and stared about me,
surprised to find myself in James's
room. He lay beside me with eyes closed, breathing
peacefully, his face pink with health.

"Miss, are you in there?" Nellie called. "Mrs.
Dawson has sent me to fetch you for supper."

James opened his eyes. "Where is Sophia?" he
asked, still groggy from sleep.

"Gone," I whispered, remembering my vision of
her vanishing among the tombstones in the churchyard, defeated forever, I hoped.

"Truly gone?" James looked doubtful.

"She's not here now, I'm certain of it."

Nellie knocked and called again.

"Who's knocking?" he asked, suddenly fearful.

"It's just Nellie," I told him.

James rubbed the sleep from his eyes. "You're certain it's not—"

I put my hand gently over his mouth. "Don't say her name."

"Tell Nellie to come in," he mumbled.

The girl entered, carrying a coal scuttle as usual. "Beg your pardon, but the fire needs tending," she said to James. To me, she said, "Be ye coming to supper, miss?"

"I am." I turned to James. "How about you? Do you feel well enough to join us?"

"If Uncle would be kind enough to carry me down. My legs are a bit shaky still."

Nellie gave him a shy smile. "It'll be a rare sight to see you at table," she told James. "Never have ye been out of yer bed since I come here."

James sat up straighter, a grin on his face. "I hope to be out and about every day, Nellie. I've stayed in this room much too long. There's more to do than lie in bed and read and sleep."

Nellie turned her attention to the fire. When she'd added coal and stirred it with a poker, she asked

James if she should ask Mr. Crutchfield to bring him down to the dining room.

James nodded. "Yes, please, Nellie."

Cheeks flushed with pleasure, Nellie darted away.

Soon Uncle appeared, a bit breathless from running up the stairs.

"Nellie tells me you wish to dine with us," he said. "Dr. Fielding advised you to rest, but if you feel strong enough, you jolly well shall join us!"

With a smile, Uncle wrapped James in a blanket and carried him downstairs. As he settled him in a comfortable chair, Aunt shot her brother a disapproving look but said nothing. Without speaking to any of us, she sat quietly, cutting her mutton into small bites, chewing slowly, and pausing now and then for a sip of water.

All around her, Uncle, James, and I talked and laughed and discussed the days that lay ahead. We did not mention the roof. We did not speak Sophia's name.

When Mrs. Dawson came to clear the table, she was humming an old song about wild mountain thyme and blooming heather. She gave us all a cheerful smile and patted James on his head.

"It's right glad I am to see you here, my boy," she said, "eating your dinner and enjoying yourself. It's as if a dark cloud has lifted and the days ahead will be bright and sunny and you'll play like the lamb you are."

James ducked his head and looked embarrassed, but I had a feeling he was glad of the happiness in Mrs. Dawson's voice. Glad to be at the table instead of in his lonely room. Glad his sister was gone.

From that night on, James's health improved quickly. Although Dr. Fielding was delighted, he couldn't explain it medically. But he was happy to attribute it to his skill.

Unfortunately, Aunt continued to compare me unfavorably to Sophia, refusing to listen to anyone else's opinion of her niece. She also considered me a bad influence on James.

"He was no trouble while he was sick," she pointed out with a frequency that quickly became monotonous. "A perfect little angel, he was, before that girl took an interest in him."

Early that spring, Aunt took it into her head to move to Eastbourne, where she shared a residence with a cousin even more disagreeable than she was—or so Mrs. Dawson claimed. No one missed her. Indeed, we were all glad she was gone.

As he'd promised, Uncle hired a governess for James and me. Miss Amelia was young and pretty and good natured. She made our lessons entertaining, and I found myself enjoying subjects I'd previously disliked. Even mathematics lost its terror.

As winter waned and the days grew longer and warmer, Miss Amelia encouraged James and me to spend more time out-of-doors. Impressed with our drawing skills, she urged us to try what she called *plein air* exercises.

"Find a tree, a building, a view," she told us, "and sit outside and sketch."

At first we were satisfied to draw the garden, the terrace, the fine old oaks lining the drive, and the distant hills. There seemed no end of interesting views to capture. Old stone walls, outbuildings, Spratt at work with hoe or shovel, Cat sleeping in the sun.

One afternoon, I was hard at work drawing the cat's ears, a very difficult thing to get right. Suddenly James sighed in exasperation and threw his pencil down.

"I'm tired of drawing that cat," he said.

"Draw something else then," I suggested. I was vexed with the cat myself. He kept changing his position, which meant everything I'd drawn before was wrong, including his dratted ears.

James looked around and frowned. "I don't see anything I want to draw."

"We could go for a walk," I said. "Maybe we'll find something new."

Gathering our pencils and sketchpads, we headed for the fields beyond the stone wall. A narrow public walkway led over a hill.

"I've been this way before," I told James.

"When?"

"I walked up the drive the day I came to Crutchfield Hall, so it couldn't have been then." I looked around, beginning to remember. "There was snow on the ground, and I was cold. The wind blew in my face. I was running."

"Were you alone?" James asked, suddenly serious.

I shook my head, remembering everything. "I was with Sophia. She took me to the churchyard to see her headstone. It was the day she made you climb out on the roof. Her death-day."

"Poor Sophia," James whispered. "She's been gone all this time, and we haven't visited her grave once."

"Do you think we should?" Truthfully, I wasn't at all certain I wanted to be that near Sophia. Suppose we disturbed her somehow? Suppose she came back?

He looked at me. "She's all alone there."

Reluctantly, I followed James up the hill, through the gate, and down the road to the village. It was a weekday, so not many people were about. A woman hung laundry in her yard. A small child pulled an even smaller child in a wagon. A horse trotted by hauling a carriage at a good clip. I glimpsed a bonneted head inside. A dog sleeping in the middle of the road got up and moved slowly out of the horse's way.

Under an almost cloudless sky, the old stone church dozed in the shade of trees. How different it had looked on that snowy day last winter, the stones dark and imposing, the trees bare, the wind howling. Now the headstones rose from freshly cut grass, tilting this way and that, some mossy with age, others newer. A flock of crows strutted among the stones, pecking in the grass. From the church roof, a line of wood pigeons watched us. Their melancholy voices blended well with the setting.

Hand in hand, James and I walked along gravel paths looking for Sophia's grave. Then we saw it. Her tilted stone cast a shadow across the grass.

In a low voice, James read his sister's inscription aloud. When he spoke her name, I braced myself, fearing she might rise up before us.

She did not appear. The wood pigeons cooed, a crow called and another answered, a breeze rustled the leaves over our heads, but Sophia remained silent.

"Do you know what today is?" James asked.

I thought for a moment. "It's the twenty-seventh of July," I whispered. "Half a year since we last saw her."

James held my hand tighter. "Do you think she'll come back again?"

"I hope not," I said, but I couldn't hide the uncertainty in my voice.

"Perhaps her spirit isn't here anymore," James said. "Perhaps she's with Mama and Papa." He looked at me as if for confirmation.

I nodded, hoping it was true.

"Maybe she's not angry now," James said softly. "Maybe she's not jealous. Maybe she knows now that she can't change her fate."

I nodded again, still hoping it was true, still not sure. Sophia was not the sort who would accept what could not be changed.

"I miss her sometimes," James said. "She wasn't always mean, you know. She could be quite nice when she wanted to be."

"I'm glad to hear that." I stared at the gravestone, warmed by the afternoon sun. It was almost impossible to picture Sophia lying peacefully six feet below us, tucked into her grave as snugly as a child is tucked into bed. All that anger, all that energy—where had it gone?

For a moment, the grass over Sophia moved as if something deep down below stirred in its sleep. With a flash of terror, I remembered what she'd told me about crawling from her grave six months after her death. I backed away, almost tripping on a tree root. *Six months*, I thought. *Six months today.*

Unaware of my distress, James contemplated Sophia's headstone. "Can we sit here for a while?" he asked. "I have a mind to draw a picture of my sister's grave."

I wanted to say no. I did not like graveyards, especially this one, but he'd already sat down and spread his art supplies on the grass.

While James sketched, I resisted the urge to seize his arm and pull him away. Perhaps I was being overly cautious, but I did not dare risk disturbing Sophia. Anything might rouse her—the scritch-scratch of James's pencil, the sad calls of the pigeons, the wind in the grass, even the soft sound of my breath or the solemn beat of my heart.

"James," I whispered. "We should go home. Uncle will wonder where we've gone."

He looked at me and smiled. "All right. I've finished my drawing."

As James gathered his things, I glanced at his picture. He'd drawn not only the tombstone, but his sister as well, standing in its shadow, blending in with the trees behind her. I couldn't be sure if she was smiling or frowning.

"Why is Sophia in the picture?" I asked him.

"She's not," he said.

I held the picture up and pointed to the indistinct image. "Who's this, then?"

James stared at what he'd drawn and shook his head. "I didn't put her there—I swear I didn't." He began to cry. "I was just sketching the trees. That's all. How did she get in my picture? Who drew her?"

I put my arms around him and stared over his head at Sophia's grave. Once again the grass stirred. A wind rose and rustled the leaves. For a moment, I thought I heard someone laughing at us.

Dropping the picture, I took James's hand. He looked at me, his face pale with fear. "Is she coming back?" he whispered.

I stared at the shadowy place under the tree, not sure whether she was there or not. "Even if she does come back," I said, "she can't hurt us. What's done is done. No matter how often she tries to change her fate, she will fail."

James tightened his grip on my hand. "It's very sad," he whispered. "I feel sorry for her."

"Better to feel sorry than frightened." Turning back to the shadowy place under the tree, I said loudly, "We are stronger than you are, Sophia. You cannot harm us, you cannot frighten us, you cannot make us obey you anymore."

"Leave us alone!" James cried. "Please, please, Sophia, rest in peace."

The wind rustled the leaves and blew through the grass on Sophia's grave. Its sound was as low and sad as the pigeons calling to one another on the church roof.

Wordlessly, James and I left the churchyard. Over our heads, the sky was a clear blue dome, and the road lay before us, dappled with sunshine and shadow. When we got home, Mrs. Dawson would have tea and cake ready for us. Later, we'd take our books outside and read in the garden or play croquet with Miss Amelia.

I looked over my shoulder. The old church spire rose above the trees. I could no longer see the graves, but I knew they were there, dozing in the sunlight, tilting this way and that, some cradled in tree roots, some almost hidden in tangles of weeds and wild-flowers. I hoped Sophia had heard what we'd said and would remain where we'd left her, at peace among the dead.